LEGENDTOPIA

The Battle for Urth

Lee Bacon

Delacorte Press

Text and map copyright © 2016 by Lee Bacon
Jacket art copyright © 2016 by Alyssa Petersen

randomhousekids.com

Educators and librarians, for a variety of teaching tools,
visit us at RHTeachersLibrarians.com

Library of Congress Cataloging-in-Publication Data
Names: Bacon, Lee, author.
Title: Legendtopia : the battle for Urth / Lee Bacon.
Other titles: Battle for Urth
Description: First edition. | New York: Delacorte Press, [2016] | Summary: A sixth-grade
girl and a prince from an enchanted kingdom join forces to battle an evil sorceress who
brings dark magic to suburbia.
Identifiers: LCCN 2015025989 | ISBN 978-0-553-53402-3 (hc) |
ISBN 978-0-553-53404-7 (ebook)
Subjects: CYAC: Magic—Fiction. | Princes—Fiction | Fantasy.
Classification: LCC PZ7.B13446 Le 2016 | DDC [Fic]—dc23

The text of this book is set in 13-point Adobe Jenson.
Interior design by Trish Parcell

Printed in the United States of America
10 9 8 7 6 5 4 3 2 1
First Edition

To all the librarians out there.
You are the magicians.
You open the doors
to a vast number of worlds.

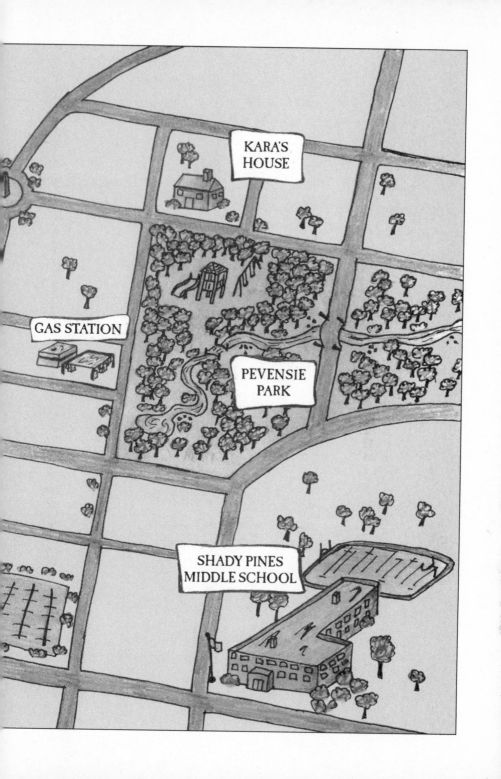

Prince Fred

Do you know the legend?

There is a legend of another world. A world of magic and wonder. A world where carriages travel without horses and winged machines fly higher than any bird. A world where all the information in all the libraries fits in the palm of your hand. A world where the light of a thousand candles can be ignited with the flick of a single switch.

A world known as Urth.

According to the legend, a doorway separates my world from Urth. A small wooden door that stands half as tall as any normal door.

But if you attempt to open the door, it refuses to budge.

Go ahead and give it another tug. It won't make the slightest difference. Because, you see, the peculiar miniature door can be opened only by someone from the other side. Someone from Urth.

Over the years, there have been countless attempts to open the door. The strongest men in the kingdom pulled it with all their might. The most powerful wizards cast their most potent spells.

None of it ever worked.

For as long as anyone can remember, the door has remained closed. Locked. A mystery.

Until the day a girl named Kara walked through and changed my life forever.

Kara

This is going to be epic.

At least, that's Marcy's opinion. She's next to me on the bus, bouncing up and down so excitedly that the entire seat shakes.

"Epic, epic, epic!" she squeals.

Today our sixth-grade English class is on its way to this fantasy-theme restaurant in town. Legendtopia. I've never been to the place before. To be honest, fantasy isn't really my thing. Marcy, on the other hand . . . She's always reading books with elves and unicorns on the covers. Her last birthday party was Hobbit themed. She spent the entire afternoon wearing fake furry feet.

For the past week, our class has been studying folklore and old myths. The lesson had something to do with heroic quests and magical creatures. Like I said, I'm not that big on fantasy. I tuned out until Mrs. Olyphant said two words that totally caught my attention:

Field trip.

I may not care much about the subject matter, but anything's better than sitting in class.

"I've been begging my parents to take me to Legendtopia for, like, ever!" Marcy grins, showing off a mouthful of braces. "But for some reason, we've never gone."

"Probably 'cause it's totally lame," says Trevor Fitzgerald from the seat in front of us.

Marcy stops bouncing and shoots Trevor a nasty glare. "How do you know?"

"I went there last summer," Trevor says. "Major letdown."

But Marcy's not having any of it. "I hear there's a dragon. And ogres that really talk." She turns to me. "Back me up, Kara? You're excited, right?"

I hesitate. "I'm excited we won't have to eat cafeteria food."

This is an understatement. Yesterday my french fries came with a side of fungus.

But my comment's not exactly a huge show of support

4

for Marcy. And now her enthusiasm's fading. She droops in her seat, arms crossed.

Even though Marcy can go a little crazy about all this fantasy stuff, I don't like seeing her disappointed. We met in the first grade. Our dance class was staging the annual holiday show *Snow White and the Seven Reindeer*. She played a chipmunk. I was a dancing bush. We've been friends ever since.

I place a hand on her shoulder. "So Legendtopia has a dragon?"

Marcy nods.

"And ogres?"

She nods again. "They talk."

"Sounds pretty epic to me."

The smile reappears on Marcy's face. "That's what I'm saying."

And just like that, she's bouncing up and down again.

While the bus rumbles across town, I look out the window and twirl my owl necklace between my fingers. It's a habit. Some people chew their nails or bite their hair. I have my necklace. The little silver owl dangles from its chain. Sunlight traces the edges of its pointy beak and perfectly round eyes.

It was a gift from my dad. The last thing he ever gave me.

The owl slips out of my fingers when the bus lurches around a corner. Suddenly, Legendtopia appears in the window. Take it from me, the place is impossible to miss. It's supposed to look like an old European castle. Except I doubt many European castles are located in shopping centers, sandwiched between a bank and Crazy Earl's Electronics Extravaganza.

Our class exits the bus and follows Mrs. Olyphant toward the restaurant. Fake stone turrets loom crookedly over the parking lot. The door is actually a small-scale drawbridge over a goldfish pond.

In the entryway, we're greeted by a suit of armor. I jump when the suit extends its arms and begins to speak. "Wruppmmh tulmphhia wurrph lurrgghh compph lippphh."

"Excuse me?" Mrs. Olyphant says.

The person in the armor raises a creaky glove and lifts away the faceplate. Inside the helmet is a pimply teenager. He repeats himself, and this time his words come out more clearly—

"Welcome to Legendtopia, where legends come to life."

The guy leads us into the restaurant. It's hard to hear exactly what he's saying—his armor makes most of the noise.

"Follow me, ladies and lords, into another world." CLANK! SQUEEEEK! "A world of enchantment." BONK! "And mystery." CLUUUNK! "Where fantasy surrounds you." SQUONK! CLACK! "Your tables are this way."

We follow the knight through an arched doorway lined with dusty plastic vines. On the way, we pass a sign that reads:

CAUTION
OGRE CROSSING

Marcy elbows Trevor. "See. Told you there were ogres."

"Ooh, I'm real scared."

"Just wait," Marcy says. "You don't wanna mess with ogres."

Their bickering comes to a halt when a hidden door squeaks open. Out pops an ogre. Even Marcy would have to admit the thing's not exactly terrifying. Not with wires sticking out of its ears and cotton stuffing poking from ripped seams.

But Marcy did at least get one thing right. The ogre *does* talk.

Sort of.

"GRRR! I WILL EAT YOUR BONES!" growls the ogre. Its electronic voice is so garbled, it sounds more like a malfunctioning toaster.

We keep moving. Marcy casts a disappointed look over her shoulder. "What kind of ogre was *that?*"

"A lame ogre!" Trevor grins triumphantly. "Just like I said."

"Whatever." I grab Marcy's arm and guide her away from Trevor. "Don't listen to him."

"He's kinda right," Marcy grumbles.

"Yeah, well . . . I bet the rest of Legendtopia is gonna be better."

But as I glance around the restaurant, I'm not so sure. Everything looks completely fake. The royal throne is made of Styrofoam. The unicorn is a stuffed horse with a horn duct-taped to its head.

Legendtopia is epic, all right.

Epic fail.

But Marcy hasn't quite given up on the place yet. She perks up when a savage roar booms through the corridor.

Up ahead, the knight clanks to a stop. "What is that noise I hear? It sounds like . . . *the dragon!*"

Marcy shoots me an excited grin. "I knew there'd be a dragon."

We both flinch at the sound of another roar. Smoke

wafts into the room. The thrill of the unknown hangs heavily in the air. The atmosphere of dangerous enchantment. This must be what Marcy enjoys about old myths and fantasy stories. The feeling that magic is real. That anything's possible.

A dark shape emerges from within the smoke. Even though I know it's fake, my heart beats a little faster. I grip Marcy's elbow a little tighter. The dark form snakes its way closer and closer through the mist, until—finally—we get a glimpse of the thing. . . .

And it doesn't look much like a dragon at all.

More like an oversized chicken.

Marcy stamps her foot. "That's not a dragon."

The only person in our group who seems afraid of the big purple chicken is the pimply knight. He draws his plastic sword and waves it around.

"Quick, let us flee this place!" *SQUEEEEK! HOINK!* "Before the dragon devours us all!"

"Yeah, let's escape the horrifying chicken puppet," Trevor jeers as we shuffle away.

For Marcy's sake, I'm hoping the show's going to improve once we get to our long wooden table. No luck there. As soon as we're seated, a lady in a pointy hat and robe barges forward.

"Greetings and salutations!" she announces. "My name

is Gerlaxia, and I am the most magical witch in all the land! I'll be your waitress today!"

The lady's hat is stained with mustard. Tennis shoes poke out from under her robe.

"Prepare yourselves for a display of stupendous sorcery and enthralling enchantment! But first—allow me to fetch your menus."

Gerlaxia twirls her hands and a bunch of menus come tumbling out of her sleeve.

"Oops," the witch mumbles.

After scooping up the menus, she begins circling our table, taking drink orders. She gets to me last. As Gerlaxia leans over, the brim of her pointy hat snags my owl necklace. When she spins to leave, the chain snaps. The necklace breaks loose, stuck in her hat.

Gerlaxia struts away, unaware that she's taking my silver owl with her.

Panic fills my voice. "My necklace!"

I try to get up from the table, but I'm wedged in. Watching the fake witch disappear from view, I feel like I just lost the last tiny bit of my dad that I had left.

"I'm sure she'll be right back," Marcy says.

"But what if it falls out!" I twist sideways, but I'm still unable to squeeze out of my seat. "I have to get it back!"

Marcy's expression sharpens. "Then you know what you need to do, right?" The lights of Legendtopia gleam in her eyes. "You have to rescue your necklace from the evil witch! It's, like, an epic quest!"

Marcy joins me in shoving our bench away from the table. And this time, the two of us manage to push hard enough for me to climb out.

"May you prevail in your quest!" Marcy calls after me.

I hurry past another animatronic ogre (this one wearing an XXL T-shirt that reads I HAD A LEGENDARY TIME AT LEGENDTOPIA). Then I catch sight of a purple robe and matching hat. The waitress pushes through a door marked MAGICAL EMPLOYEES ONLY. I race to follow her, but the door's being guarded by an elf. And by "elf," I mean a guy with fake pointy ears.

"You can't go in there," the elf says in a bored voice.

"I just need to get something from our waitress," I explain. "She walked through this door like two seconds ago. Remember? The witch?"

The elf points at the sign. "Sorry. Magical employees only."

I clench my hands into fists. Gerlaxia is getting away. And so is my necklace.

All of a sudden, the door swings open and the knight

emerges. Turning his attention to the elf, he says, "Some lady just spilled nachos on the unicorn. Manager wants you to scrub it off."

I don't hear the rest of their conversation. Because as the door swings closed, I slip inside. I seem to be in some kind of backstage area. There are shelves of costumes and wigs. A pile of fake vines. Papier-mâché fairies dangle from the ceiling, suspended by fishing line.

I bolt into the next room. The kitchen. Crouching low, I scurry past sizzling pans and smoking ovens. The door opens behind me. The elf and knight stumble into the kitchen.

I dart behind a humongous silver box. On the door is a sign that reads:

WALK-IN REFRIGERATOR
BUSTED

It's definitely the biggest fridge I've ever seen. Big enough to hide in. I tug open the door and slip through the opening. The inside looks like a big metal closet, with empty shelves and the remains of old food scattered around. I guess it's been unplugged for a long time, because it isn't cold at all.

And something else I notice about the walk-in refrigerator: the entire space smells like spoiled vegetables.

Yuck.

But it looks like I'll have to put up with the smell. At least long enough to avoid getting caught by the knight and the elf.

I pull the door the rest of the way closed. Everything goes pitch-black.

In the darkness, my imagination conjures the owl necklace. Big silver eyes and little pointed beak. I remember the night Dad gave it to me. I was eight. At the time, it seemed strange that he was giving me a present. It wasn't my birthday or Christmas or any other special occasion. When I pointed this out to Dad, he pulled the jewelry away.

"Maybe you're right," he said. His accent made the words come out almost musical. Every sentence sounded like it might break into a tango party. "I should probably wait."

He pretended to stick the necklace back into his pocket.

"Noooo!" I squealed, reaching for it.

Dad smiled. He had the kind of smile that made all the lightbulbs in the room glow a little brighter. "All right, *hija*. Why don't you try it on?"

As he clasped the necklace around my neck, I could smell a mixture of oil and charred wires. Dad was an electrician. When he got home from work, he would sometimes drop his toolbox on the living room floor and put on a show for the family. With the twist of a screwdriver, he could make a circuit board hum a Frank Sinatra tune. Or he might cause magnets to twirl and float above our rug. Pressing two wires together, he'd create sparks that turned our coffee table into a miniature Fourth of July fireworks display.

These shows usually went on either until bedtime or until the couch caught on fire—whichever came first.

But on the night Dad gave me the necklace, there was no toolbox, and there were no tricks. Just the little silver owl dangling from a chain.

"It's beautiful," I said.

"So are you, *hija*." Dad smiled. The lights glowed so bright, I thought they might explode. "If you keep this necklace with you, it'll bring you closer to me."

I didn't know it then, but it was the last time I would ever see him. The next day, Dad went off to work. And never came back.

That was more than three years ago. I've worn the owl necklace ever since. There are moments when I can almost feel its little metal wings fluttering against my skin. When I hold it tightly and imagine that my dad is still with me.

And now it could be anywhere. Dropped into someone's soup or snagged on a unicorn's horn. Accidentally tossed into the trash or kicked under a toilet in the restroom.

Gone.

I can't let that happen. I have to get out of this refrigerator.

As my eyes adjust to the darkness, I notice the light.

A faint, flickering glow from the far end of the walk-in refrigerator.

Maybe it's another way out.

I begin crawling toward it. Pushing aside a cardboard box full of moldy lemons, I see the light shining brighter. I have to hunch to fit underneath a shelf, like climbing into a cave.

Suddenly, a chill prickles my skin. When I entered the fridge, everything had been made of steel. But now, the cramped walls seem to be . . . brick.

Up ahead, I spot the source of the light. And I can barely believe my eyes. Flaming torches. They're attached to the brick wall. And between them, there's . . .

A door.

A small wooden door.

Some major questions pop up in my brain. Where is this tunnel leading me? What's behind the door? And how big is this walk-in refrigerator, anyway?

I creep forward until I'm close enough to feel the heat coming off the torches. The fire jumps and flickers. My shadow dances on the brick wall.

The door is right in front of me. The torches hiss and murmur. Almost like they're whispering, *Go ahead. Turn the handle.*

And so I do.

The small door creaks open.

I crouch close to the ground and step inside.

Prince Fred

⌒

Allow me to properly introduce myself.

My name is Frederick Alexander Siegfried Maria Thorston XIV, Prince of the Realm and Heir to the Throne of Heldstone. But if you prefer, you may simply call me Prince Frederick the Fourteenth.

And please—I must insist—do *not* call me Prince Fred.

The day begins like most others. In the morning, my many servants assist in getting me dressed. They deposit me into my stockings, button my waistcoat, and tie the ribbons on my silken slippers. This is followed by an hour of grooming. Carefully plucking my eyebrows, buffing my fingernails, styling my hair.

It's not easy to look as regal and handsome as I do.

After dismissing my servants, I stand alone by my bedchamber window for a moment. Pushing away the velvet curtains, I gaze out upon the Forest of Enchantment. Vast and green. At night, the trees dance with one another like guests in a ballroom.

To the east, the primitive mud dwellings of Grok, where thousands of trolls make their homes. To the west, Valpathia, the capital city of Heldstone. The sun gleams off the towering monuments and grand houses.

Heldstone is bustling with activity. A horse-drawn carriage clatters past a family of witches selling counterfeit potions on the side of the road. A mother dragon swoops through the sky. She is trailed by three baby dragons still clumsy in flight. Below, a line of knights returns from battle. Merchants carry their goods in wooden carts. Elves argue with dwarfs about who-knows-what.

It is truly a marvelous kingdom. I look forward to ruling it someday.

———

The palace is a hive of activity. Tomorrow is the start of the Luminary Ball, the grandest celebration of the decade. Seven days of parades, feasts, and dancing. Everyone is busy preparing. Washerwomen shake out the silken sheets, servants dust the priceless furniture. But the staff scatters at the sound of sharp footsteps on the marble floor. A moment later, I see the cause of their sudden escape.

The Sorceress.

She appears from around a corner. Her long, dark hair blends seamlessly with her long, dark dress. Skin as pale as glaciers. Lips the color of blood.

If the Sorceress has a name, nobody in the palace knows it. For years, she has served as the Royal Wizardess, the most powerful magician in the entire kingdom. She is beautiful. Stunningly beautiful. Unnaturally beautiful. As if her features have been carved from marble by the kingdom's most talented artists.

She also has a terrifying temper. Which is probably why the servants went running at the sound of her footsteps.

And one other thing about the Sorceress: she despises me.

As the Royal Prince of the Realm, I'm unaccustomed to being disliked. Everyone else in the kingdom seems rather fond of me. Whenever I stand upon the terrace to toss gold coins over the palace walls, people cheer. Whenever I ask my servants' opinions about me, they're always quite flattering.

"Am I a dignified prince?" I ask.

"You are the noblest prince in the history of the kingdom," my servants inevitably reply.

"Yes, but am I brave as well?"

"Your courage is without equal, Your Highness."

"Perhaps I am eating too much. Lately I have noticed that I look a bit . . . pudgy."

"Don't even think it, Prince Frederick! You are the most elegant boy who ever lived!"

See what I mean? Everyone loves me!

Except the Sorceress.

Perhaps it has something to do with an incident that occurred several weeks ago. I was returning from an afternoon lesson with the Royal Tutor when I noticed the doorway to the Chamber of Wizardry. It was open a crack. I'd never seen this before. Ordinarily, the Sorceress keeps the door locked at all times.

My curiosity ignited like a torch. I quietly approached the thick oaken door and peered inside.

The Chamber of Wizardry was crammed with all manner of magical instruments and peculiar objects. And at the other end of the room was the Sorceress. She had her back to me, hunched on the floor beside a burbling brass urn. In front of her was the door.

The miniature wooden door.

The door to Urth.

Reaching inside the urn, the Sorceress scooped out a handful of bubbling, smoking liquid. She smeared the substance upon the tiny door handle.

I leaned forward. Would it work? Would this be the fateful moment that the mythical door opened at last? Would the Sorceress finally—

CLUMP!

I must've been leaning a little too far into the room. For at that moment, I slipped forward and fell into the Chamber of Wizardry.

The disturbance startled the Sorceress. She knocked the urn onto its side. Toxic green liquid spilled everywhere, hissing and dissolving the floorboards.

The Sorceress whirled to face me. Her pale features wrenched in anger. "What are you doing in my chambers, you spoiled little worm?" she screamed.

I scrambled to my feet and raced out of the room. Down the hall and as far from the Chamber of Wizardry as I could.

Ever since, I've done everything I can to avoid the Sorceress.

Until now.

Until this very moment.

The Sorceress is walking toward me. Her dress drifts behind her like a shadow.

My heart thunders inside my chest. I feel a rising fear that she'll cast an evil spell on me. What if broccoli sprouts from my nostrils? Or she turns my head into a troll's bottom?

But none of that happens. Instead, the Sorceress's beautiful lips form into a beautiful smile. She bows. And in a polite, respectful voice, she says, "Good morning, Your Highness. You look magnificent as ever."

At the same time, a voice rings inside my ears. A voice that comes from nowhere and everywhere. The Sorceress's voice. And inside my head, her words echo.

Your punishment will soon come, you spoiled little worm.

I'm left standing there. Stunned. Impossible to say exactly how much time passes. A minute? An hour? I return to my senses only when my parents appear in the hallway. They look as elegant as their portraits, which hang throughout the palace. Diamonds and rubies twinkle in Father's crown. Beside him, Mother is draped in a violet-feathered gown.

"Ah, Frederick! There you are!" Mother runs a bejeweled hand through my hair. "But shouldn't you be at tutoring by now?"

"Tutoring?" I feel as though the Sorceress has emptied the contents of my brain. It takes another moment to remember what I was doing before my encounter with her. "The knights. They're training in the courtyard. I was hoping to join them."

Mother sniffs derisively. "Why would you want to do such a thing?"

"To practice my swordsmanship."

Father frowns. "I don't believe that's a wise idea."

"Nor do I," says Mother.

My shoulders slump. "You don't?"

"You are young," says Father. "And swords are dangerous."

"We cannot risk our only son getting injured," says Mother.

I look from Mother to Father pleadingly. "But how will I ever learn?"

"Leave the swords and shields to the knights," says Father.

Mother pats my head. "You are a prince. You are destined to *command* armies. Not fight in them. Now hurry along. The Royal Tutor is awaiting you."

There's no point in drawing out the debate. When your parents are king and queen, they win every argument.

I enter the Royal Tutor's chambers. The ancient man is seated with his back to me. Wispy strands of his white hair shimmer in the candlelight. He's hunched over a knotted oaken table, one wrinkled hand resting on a tattered piece of parchment.

As I approach, I peer over the tutor's shoulder to gain a better glimpse. He appears to be reading some kind of poem. Looping script, written in dark ink . . .

From a distant, unknown land came he.
A Traveler he claimed to be.
People flocked, far and wide, to listen
To the fantastical tales of the Elektro-Magician.

There's more to the poem, but it's blocked by the tutor's shoulder. As I take another step into the room, the floorboard creaks under my foot and the old man stirs. He turns the parchment over.

"Prince Frederick!" The tutor rises unsteadily to his feet and gazes at me with milky eyes. "I didn't hear you come in!"

"What are you reading?"

"Nothing that should concern you, sire." The old fellow pats the overturned parchment. "Your father's spies intercepted a message being passed among the Thurphen-wald tribe."

"The poem is about a Traveler. Do you think he's from Urth?"

The tutor's slender chest rises and falls. "Urth is not the subject of today's lesson."

"But it's behind that door. The little wooden door. Is it not?"

"That is what the legend claims."

"Please. Tell me more."

The old man sighs. "According to the legend, Urth isn't cubical. It is perfectly round. Like a marble. The inhabitants of Urth do not fight their battles with swords and axes. Instead, they use—"

"Sticks that shoot fire!" I say eagerly. I have heard this story many times before.

"That is correct."

"And what about the magical pipes?"

"Ah, yes. Those. Instead of warming themselves by the fire when they become cold, the people of Urth press a switch that releases warm air from magical pipes. Or by turning the switch another way, the air can become very cold."

"I want to go to Urth!"

The tutor shakes his head. "I'm afraid that is impossible."

"But what about the poem?" I point at the parchment. "It claims that the Elektro-Magician—"

"Enough about the Elektro-Magician. It is past time to begin today's lesson."

I groan. The tutor heaves a thick, dusty book from the shelf and drops it onto the table.

Right on top of the parchment.

"We will be continuing our lesson in genealogical history." The tutor opens the book to an etching of a man. In the picture, a sword is hoisted above the man's crowned head. "This is King Frederick the Ninth. Your great-great-great grandfather. Also known as King Frederick the Fierce. He single-handedly slew fifteen trolls during the Battle of Broggincout."

The tutor turns the page.

"And this is King Frederick the Eighth. Your great-great-great-great grandfather. Commonly known as King Frederick the Giant Killer. It was during his reign that the giants became extinct. . . ."

While the tutor wheezes about genealogical history, I listen to the sounds coming from outside. The clash of steel against steel. Grunts and cheers and laughter. Glancing out the window, I look down upon the knights who are training in the courtyard.

If only I could join them!

How will I ever live up to the greatness of my brave ancestors if I spend all my days with an old tutor, enduring one tedious lesson after another? Did King Frederick the Fierce gain his talents for troll slaying in the Hall of Learning? Did King Frederick the Giant Killer sharpen his fighting skills in the pages of dusty old books?

Of course not!

I turn away from the window. My attention shifts back to the tutor.

"... which brings us to your great-great-great-great-great-great-great-great-great-great grandfather. Remembered now as King Frederick the Bold. It is said that he wrestled bears for his own amusement. When he fell in love with a mermaid, he taught himself to breathe underwater in order to be closer to her...."

A wave of jealousy washes over me. How will I ever match the achievements of my troll-fighting, giant-killing, bear-wrestling, mermaid-loving forebearers? My parents won't allow me to train with swords. The tutor refuses to tell me more about Urth. And if I get anywhere near the miniature door, the Sorceress will probably turn my hair into seaweed!

If things continue the way they are, I'll spend the rest of my life locked away behind the thick walls of this palace.

Safe and well-groomed . . .

And bored out of my skull.

Which is why—when the lesson finally comes to an end—I wait until the tutor is distracted before slipping a hand under the heavy book. In a single motion, I remove the tattered parchment and place it in my pocket.

Kara

I'm in some kind of medieval science lab. Surrounded by jars of colorful powders and ancient scrolls. A cauldron bubbles and smokes. A flickering candle casts its light onto a globe—except that, instead of being round, this globe is shaped like a cube. And when I lean in for a closer look, I don't recognize a single one of the continents.

Then again, geography has never been my strongest subject.

Nearby is a grandfather clock with thirteen numbers around its face. Aren't there supposed to be *twelve*? The room is warmed by a crackling fire with flames that change colors, from purple to green to blue.

There's a skeleton hanging from a wooden rack. It looks

like the kind of thing you'd see in a science textbook, but with one huge difference: the skull only has one eye, a gaping hole right in the center of its forehead.

The outlandish strangeness of everything makes my head spin. Then I remind myself . . . *It's just another part of Legendtopia.*

When I wandered through the miniature door, I must've entered a different section of the restaurant. And I've gotta say—they did a *way* better job on this area. Unlike the cheesy fake-castle decorations I passed by earlier, everything in here looks . . . *real.*

Beside me, a rickety wooden desk is covered with a tattered scroll. On top of the scroll is a little glass jar of ink. A long feather quill pokes out of the jar. I reach for the quill. My fingers are closing around the feather when I hear a woman's voice—

"Hello, little girl."

I spin around. The entrance to the lab is open. Not the small door I came through, but a normal-sized door at the other end of the room.

And standing in the doorway is the most beautiful woman I've ever seen.

She's very tall and very slender, with skin so pale it seems to glow. Her black hair drapes over her shoulders, blending into the pattern of her black dress so that you can't tell where one ends and the other begins.

"Are you enjoying snooping around the Chamber of Wizardry?" she asks in an English accent.

"I'm sorry," I say. "I just got lost."

The woman smiles, but there's nothing friendly about her. "Lost?"

She moves toward me, until she's looming over me. I feel like someone just cranked up the AC. A chill runs down my neck.

"How did you get in here?" she asks.

"I came through the door."

"Which door?"

I point at the miniature door that I pulled closed on my way into the room. "That one."

The woman inhales a sharp breath. "You came from . . . the other side?"

"Yeah, I guess." I shrug. "The other side of the restaurant."

"You're not lying to me, are you, little girl?"

I shake my head.

The woman stares at me. "That explains your curious accent," she whispers, as though speaking to herself, not me. "And your bizarre clothing. You've come from . . . *Earth*."

She has a weird way of pronouncing the word "Earth." It sounds more like "Urth."

Maybe on another trip, the whole magical-evil-lab-experience might actually be worth visiting. But right now, I have more important things to deal with. Like finding my necklace and getting back to our class before Mrs. Olyphant gets seriously angry.

Besides, this lady's really starting to creep me out. Her eyes are dark and filled with greed. The way she's looking at me makes me feel like a fly caught in a spider's web.

And she's the spider.

"So, uh . . . ," I say in a shaky voice. "I should probably get going."

But the woman only shakes her head. "You are not going anywhere," she says. "Not unless you take me with you."

Strands of black hair stretch across her pale skin, tentacles swimming in icy water. She no longer looks beautiful.

She looks scary.

I take a step backward, but that's as far as I get. With a flicker of movement, the woman points her pale hand toward the one-eyed skeleton. A deafening *CRAAAACK!* shreds my eardrums. A streak of white electricity jolts from the woman's fingers and collides with the one-eyed skeleton.

And all of a sudden, the skeleton begins to move.

Its chalk-white arms shake into motion. Its bony legs clatter as it steps out of the wooden rack. It turns to gaze at me with its one empty eye.

Fear and disbelief swirl inside me. The Cyclops skeleton just came to life. Like, *really* came to life. This isn't some cheesy puppet. There aren't any strings. No animatronic programming.

All of this—the magician's workshop, the one-eyed skeleton, the scary witch lady . . .

It's all real.

I flinch when a hand grips my arm. White fingers are wrapped around my wrist. I tilt my gaze upward to see a one-eyed skull leering back at me.

I try to pull away, but it's impossible to break the skeleton's grasp. Panic surges through me. Choking back tears, I turn to the pale woman.

"Wh-why are you doing this?" The words quaver as they leave my lips. "Wh-what do you want?"

The woman's dark eyes flick across the room. Toward the small wooden door. And when she speaks, her voice is cold and terrifying.

"I want you to take me to your world."

Prince Fred

I race out of the Hall of Learning with the poem in my waistcoat. Perhaps it's not very princely of me to say so, but the small act of thievery has lifted my spirits. When I reach the stairwell, I slide down the golden banister. Servants and groomsmen bow as I zip past them.

At the bottom of the stairs is the baker's apprentice, carrying a tray of bread. As I approach, he lowers his head respectfully.

And I snatch a loaf of bread off his tray.

The loaf is warm and crispy and nearly as long as my arm. I grip it tightly and swing it with all my might. It isn't quite a sword, but apparently it's as close as I'll get.

Spinning around, I jab my bread sword, knocking a bowl of grapes off the dining room table.

"Die, foul beast!" I declare. Grapes roll onto the floor.

I enter the hallway, swinging and thrusting the bread sword. Suddenly, enemies are everywhere. In my imagination, my surroundings change into a battlefield. Furnishings transform into a rampaging army. A plush armchair becomes a vicious little dwarf with a battle-ax. A tapestry on the wall looks like a horde of ogres.

And the enemies just keep coming. Twirling to the side, I defend myself against a statue, behead a vase of flowers, and severely injure a candlestick holder.

"Nobody can defeat Prince Frederick the Fourteenth!" I bellow triumphantly. "The greatest swordsman in the entire—*oof!*"

Before I know what's happening, I'm tumbling onto the carpet. Glancing back, I see what tripped me.

Xyler.

I should mention Xyler is a cat.

A cat with a habit of getting tangled in my feet.

"Xyler!" I groan. "What in the seven moons are you doing?"

The cat's eyes land on the bread sword that I'm hugging against my chest. "I might ask you the same question, Your Highness."

I look down at the bread. A few crumbs are stuck to my waistcoat. "I'm just . . . having a bite to eat."

It's obvious that Xyler doesn't believe my lie. But I'm the prince, and he spends most of his time either napping or licking himself. So he lets the matter drop.

"Of course, Your Highness," Xyler says. "I suppose you're busy preparing for the Luminary Ball?"

"Yes. Extremely busy." I climb to my feet, dusting away the crumbs. "I should probably be going."

"Enjoy the bread, Your Highness," Xyler replies.

Once I'm alone again, I return to the battle. Roaming the palace, I bravely fight off all the furnishings, paintings, and decorations that dare stand in my path. As I make my way down the corridor, I hear a woman's harsh scream echo through the palace.

"Get her! Do not let her escape!"

The voice belongs to the Sorceress. And it's followed by a cacophony of footsteps. A moment later, a figure turns the corner.

A very strangely dressed girl.

She seems to be running for her life.

Kara

⁓

The boy looks like he's from another century. He's wearing a flowery vest over a puffy white shirt with big floppy sleeves. Gold buttons run down the front of his purple coat. Instead of pants, he's in gray tights. On his feet are shiny slippers and in his hand is a baguette.

But there's one thing about the boy that stands out most of all.

We're about to run into each other.

A minute ago, I was trapped inside the room with the creepy witch lady and her skeleton sidekick. The one-eyed skeleton grabbed my wrist. Its bony feet clicked eerily against the tiles as it pulled me toward the miniature door.

Click.

Click.

Click.

I had to do something. Had to figure out a way to escape. As we passed the big wooden desk, I noticed the feather quill. The one I'd been fiddling with before the witch entered the room. Lunging sideways, I grabbed the feather with my free hand. And before the witch could react, I stabbed her with the quill's sharp point.

"Aaaagh!" She staggered backward.

The pain must've broken her spell, because the one-eyed skeleton immediately loosened its grip.

Before either of them could recover, I took off running. The witch was blocking my path to the miniature door, so I went in the opposite direction. The arched wooden doorway that she'd entered through.

As I sped toward the exit, I heard the witch's voice.

"Get her!" she shrieked. "Do not let her escape!"

This was followed by the quick clatter of bone feet against the floor. It sounded like the skeleton was gaining on me.

I spun through the door and into a fancy hallway that was lined with gold-framed paintings and the kind of furniture you see only in museums. Not that I was paying much attention to the decorating scheme. I was way too busy running for my life.

Turning a corner, I spotted him—

The boy in the fancy old-fashioned clothing.

And that's the moment when we collide.

Staggering backward, the boy gives me an infuriated look. "What in the seven moons is the meaning of this?" He has the same English accent as the witch. He peers over my shoulder just as the skeleton appears in the hall. "And why are you being chased by a one-eyed skeleton?"

I do my best to reply between gulping breaths. "No time to explain." *Gasp.* "We should run." *Wheeze.* "Now!"

"Nonsense." The boy levels a haughty gaze at the skeleton. "I command you to stop running at once."

The one-eyed skeleton keeps running.

The boy stomps his foot like a child who's not used to being ignored. "I said *stop!*"

The skeleton doesn't stop.

All of a sudden, the boy's expression changes. The arrogance and anger vanish from his features. Now he looks surprised. And afraid. The skeleton's click-clacking footsteps grow louder and louder. Its skull face grins wickedly. Any chance of escaping is long gone. So instead, I grab a heavy ceramic vase off its marble stand.

As I raise the vase above my head, the boy gasps.

"Be careful with that!" he snaps. "It's a priceless artifa—"

SMASH!

I slam the vase into the skeleton. Ceramic shards and disconnected bones explode everywhere.

"Mother loved that vase," the boy mutters.

"We'll worry about your mom later," I say. "Right now, I need a place to hide."

"Hide? From whom?"

Fear twists inside my chest. "From *her.*"

The boy follows my gaze to the end of the hall. The witch. Any trace of the beautiful woman I first encountered is gone. Her black hair tangles around her pale face like a nest of thorns. Her high cheekbones look as sharp as daggers. Her blood-red lips are twisted with rage as her shriek echoes through the hall.

"You will take me to your world, or you will *suffer!*" She thrusts out a hand, aiming her pale fingers.

CRAAAACK!

White light rushes toward me. The boy grabs a gold-framed mirror off the wall and we duck behind it. In the next instant, the light collides with the mirror.

We tumble backward. The spell reflects in the other direction . . . and smacks the witch in the stomach. She collapses.

40

Huddled behind the mirror, the boy and I peer at the Sorceress. She's sprawled out on the floor, her mouth frozen in an expression of pain. The only sign that she's still alive is the rise and fall of her chest.

Beside me, the boy stands. "Well, that was certainly . . ." His voice cracks. "Unexpected."

"That thing you did with the mirror," I begin. "Knocking the witch out with her own spell—that was brilliant."

The boy glances at the mirror in his hands like he's seeing it for the first time. "Uh . . . yes, of course. Just as I planned."

He sets the mirror down gently among the chaos of ceramic shards and one-eyed-skeleton bones. Then he turns his attention to me.

"What is your name?" he asks.

"Kara. Kara Estrada."

"It's a pleasure meeting you, Kara Estrada. My name is Frederick Alexander Siegfried Maria Thorston the Fourteenth, Prince of the Realm."

"Prince? Like, a *real* prince?"

"Of course. Surely you've heard of me!"

"Actually, I haven't. But I'm kinda new here. And to be honest, your name isn't exactly easy to remember. I bet most people just call you Prince Fred?"

The boy stares back at me. "Nobody has *ever* called me that."

I cast a nervous look at the unconscious witch. "Who *is* she, anyway?"

"The Sorceress. She's the highest-ranking, most powerful magician in the entire kingdom. She may be the most sinister as well."

"Yeah, I got that impression."

"Why was she attacking you?"

"She didn't really give much of an explanation. Something about taking her to my world."

"Your world?"

"I don't know how it happened. One minute I was crawling around in a smelly refrigerator. And the next— I was here."

The prince's mouth hangs open. "What is a refrigerator?"

"You know what—it doesn't really matter." I begin walking back the way I came. "It was nice meeting you, Prince Fred. And thanks for helping me. I really do appreciate it. But I need to get going."

"Going?" the prince calls after me. "Where?"

"Back to my world."

I hurry past the unconscious Sorceress and into her evil science lab. All I want is to get out of this place.

Behind me, I hear the prince running to catch up.

"This world that you come from. Is it called . . . *Earth?*" He has the same weird way of pronouncing "Earth" that the Sorceress had. "I've heard the legend."

My gaze shifts from Prince Fred to the miniature doorway. "Look, this has been . . . interesting. I wish I could stick around a little longer. But I don't want anything to do with the Sorceress. Besides . . ." My hand drifts up to my throat. "I lost something on the other side of that door. Something important to me. I need to get it back."

I begin moving toward the door again. But I freeze when Prince Fred speaks up.

"I'm coming with you!" he declares.

I turn to face him. "You've got to be joking."

"This is no jest. I intend to go with you."

"But you're a prince. You live in a castle. Your life must be awesome."

He shakes his head. "A prince should be bold and courageous. Nobody in this palace allows me to be either of those things. Perhaps in your kingdom, everything will be different."

"It's not a kingdom," I point out. "It's just a normal boring town."

"Regardless. I must see Urth for myself!"

"What if you get stuck there? What if you can't get back?"

"That's a risk I have to accept." He nods once, clenching his jaw. "If I'm to have a life worthy of my ancestors' great achievements, then I must go through that door. There's no other way."

I let out a sigh. "Fine. Whatever. Just as long as we get out of here before the Sorceress wakes up."

I pull the latch and the small wooden door creaks open. Prince Fred lets out a gasp. Then he follows me through the opening.

Unfortunately, neither of us thinks to close the door behind us.

Hunched forward in the confined tunnel, I run as quickly as I can without banging my head. Behind me, I can hear Prince Fred shuffling to keep up. Little by little, the light of the torches fades into darkness and the bricks become stainless steel. Soon enough, I get my first whiff of rotten vegetables.

I never thought I'd be so happy to smell something so stinky.

I push a few boxes aside, stumbling into the main part of the fridge. It's nearly pitch-black by now. I reach into my pocket and pull out my phone. Swipe, tap. The flashlight activates. A bright glow illuminates the inside of the refrigerator.

Prince Fred trips over a box and tumbles into me. "What manner of wizardry is this?"

"It's not wizardry," I say. "It's a cell phone."

"Cell ... phone." He pronounces each word like he's never heard it before. Which I guess he hasn't. "It's marvelous."

In the light of the phone, the prince looks around at the metal shelves and the old cardboard boxes.

"Where are we?" he asks.

"A walk-in refrigerator. I don't know how it happened, or why, but it seems to be some kind of portal. Between your world and mine. When we go through that door"—I point with the phone—"we'll be in my world."

What happens then? I mean, the guy looks and talks like something straight out of an old book of fairy tales. I can't imagine he'll fit in too well in Shady Pines.

But he also saved my life. If it hadn't been for his mirror trick, I would've been blasted by the spell. If Prince Fred wants to be a tourist in Shady Pines for a little while, then I'll do what I can to help him. I owe him that, at least.

"You ready?" I ask.

The prince takes a deep breath. "Absolutely."

"All right, then. Let's go."

I push open the door and we step into the kitchen. So far, so good. The cooks have their backs turned to us. And there's no sign of the employees who chased me here.

"Just keep down," I whisper. "And try not to get—"

"Hey, you kids!"

Noticed.

The elf is looking right at us. "Hey, Lenny! I found 'em!"

The scrawny teenage knight comes stumbling into the kitchen, a riot of clanking armor. "You're in big trouble, kid!" *CLANK! BONK!* "You'd better have a good excuse."

What am I supposed to say? *Sorry, but after you guys chased me into this walk-in refrigerator, I got transported to another world. There was an evil witch, a one-eyed skeleton, a prince—I barely made it out alive.*

Does that count as an excuse?

The knight points his clunky glove at Prince Fred. "Who the heck is this?"

Standing up very straight, the prince adjusts his coat. "My name is Frederick Alexander Siegfried Maria Thorston the Fourteenth, Prince of the Realm. I am a visitor to your world. I passed through an enchanted—"

"Uh . . . he's kidding," I interrupt. "Actually, he . . . he *works* here."

The elf wrinkles his forehead. "Isn't he a little young to have a job?"

"It's a work-study program," I blurt out. "He just started. Isn't that right, Fred?"

I nudge him with my elbow, hoping he'll play along. He doesn't.

"'That most certainly is *not* correct!" He stomps his foot. "I am no mere kitchen servant! My mother and father are king and queen of Heldstone!"

"Ha ha!" Even though I'm beginning to lose my patience with Prince Fred, I put on a big fake smile. "He's hilarious! Already in character."

The knight and the elf look seriously confused. But they've suddenly dropped to the bottom of my stuff-to-worry-about list. Because right then, I hear a *click* and a *clump* behind us. I spin to look back at the walk-in refrigerator just as the door swings open.

A shape moves in the darkness of the open fridge. A pale face and two deep-black eyes.

Looks like the Sorceress woke up from her nap.

And she followed us back.

Prince Fred

Urth is strange. We have entered a large kitchen. Food simmers on stoves. Pots and pans are everywhere. And roaming through the kitchen is an extremely peculiar duo.

An elf and a knight.

Except I can't help noticing that the knight is not at all knightly. More like a splotchy teenager with a weak excuse for a mustache. Next to him is the strangest elf I've ever seen. His ears are misshapen and false-looking. In his hand is a cooking instrument.

I'm still trying to make sense of all this when our odd group is joined by a most unwelcome visitor.

The Sorceress.

Her dark gaze lands upon the new surroundings. When she speaks, her voice is soft, and yet it seems to shake the entire room.

"So this is Urth?" she breathes with astonishment. "I like it. I believe I shall make it my own."

I turn a quivering glance in Kara's direction. "Did you forget to close the door?"

"You were the last one through," she hisses. "Why didn't *you* close it?"

I shrug. "My servants always close the door for me."

"Come now, little children," the Sorceress interjects. A smile cracks her blood-red lips. "There is no point arguing. You shall both be dead soon enough, anyway."

Raising one hand, she points at the oven beside us.

CRAAAACK!

A beam of light bursts from the Sorceress's hand and collides with the oven. An instant later, the oven undergoes a disturbing transformation.

It comes to life.

The oven clanks across the floor. Turning to face us, its front door flaps open. A massive flame bursts out.

Our group scatters. Kara and I escape in one direction. The elf flees in the other. And the knight falls into a pathetic metal clump behind a counter.

"Oh, man!" he whines. "I don't wanna die!"

I duck beside him. "Why are you hiding? What kind of knight are you, anyway?"

"I'm not a knight!" he cries. "It's just a part-time job."

His words make no sense. "If you're not going to fight, then give me your sword!"

"Whatever, dude." With a shrug, the knight unsheathes his sword and hands it to me. Then he rises to his feet and awkwardly clangs out of the room.

"Enough hiding, children." The Sorceress's voice echoes through the kitchen, making it impossible to know just where she is. "Come out and face me."

Gripping the sword's hilt, I turn to Kara. She's hiding behind more kitchen equipment.

"We must fight the Sorceress!" I say. "Before she wreaks further havoc!"

Kara shoots me a stupefied look. "Are you crazy? No way I'm fighting that crazy witch. Let's run while we have a chance."

"A true knight never runs from danger." I raise the sword. I'm about to charge when I notice something strange. My weapon weighs almost nothing. "Why is this sword so light?"

"Because it's not real. It's plastic."

"Plastic? What's *that?*" I wave the flimsy weapon from side to side. It would do as much good in battle as the bread sword. "It feels like a toy."

"It *is* a toy."

"But why would a knight have a toy sword?"

Kara never has a chance to answer this question. For in that moment, the oven scoots into view.

"Run!" Kara screams.

I drop the toy sword and take Kara's advice. We race out of the kitchen, flames licking at our heels. But as soon as we reach the next room, I'm attacked by fairies. An entire mob of them flaps around my face.

"Aaaaagh!" I scream. "The tiny devils are attempting to eat my brain!"

I flail and swing at the horrible fairies for another second before realizing . . . they aren't real. They're made of hard paper and are attached to clear threads that hang from the ceiling.

"They're fake!" Kara says. "Made of papier-mâché."

What's she talking about? Why would someone string fake fairies from the ceiling? As I survey the room, I notice other strange sights. A shelf labeled PROPS is strewn with all manner of wigs and weaponry. A pile of fake vines lies on the floor. A box marked DRAGON PUPPET contains a lump of fabric that resembles neither a dragon nor a puppet.

"Where *are* we?" I ask.

"Backstage." Kara points to a door at the other end of the room. "Come on! That way!"

We're halfway to the door when a jolt of light shoots past and hits the plastic vines. All of a sudden, the vines uncoil like snakes. They climb the wall and slither across the doorway, completely blocking our exit.

From the other doorway, the Sorceress speaks. Her voice is musical and sweet, but her words are quite the opposite. "I will enjoy watching you suffer, Prince. Now that you no longer have your father and his guards for protection, you will finally see the truth—you are weak. And I am powerful."

The Sorceress points at the paper fairies and releases another burst of magic. And with that, my earlier fear becomes a reality. The flock of fairies springs to life. Their skin begins to glow. Their small paper heads turn to face us. With flapping wings, the monster fairies yank free of their tethers and fly in our direction. In an instant, they're pulling at my hair and kicking me in the chin.

There's no time to hesitate. I lunge for the shelf, searching for a suitable weapon. But it's just like with the knight's sword. Everything here is a toy. There's a flimsy dagger. A battle-ax that weighs nothing. Finally, my grip lands on a pair of scissors. Not exactly what I had in mind, but at least they're solid and sharp.

I plunge the scissors into the wall of vines—once, twice, *thrice*—slashing at the enchanted plants until I manage to cut an opening big enough for us to escape through. Kara's the first through the gap. I'm about to join her when—

CRAAAACK!

Another burst of light hits the dragon puppet. All at once, the box bursts apart and its contents begin to grow.

And grow.

And *grow*.

Broad, leathery wings stretch across the room. Eyes look down on me with pure hatred.

I shiver with fear. The lump of fabric has become a scale-covered, smoke-breathing, sharp-clawed dragon.

Kara

The dragon definitely doesn't look like a chicken anymore.

Prince Fred gawks up at the massive creature like he's waiting for an introduction. Lunging through the vines, I grab Fred by the collar and yank him behind me. The dragon roars. From its open jaws comes a wave of fire that engulfs the vines.

Prince Fred and I burst into the restaurant.

All around me are tables crowded with people eating their lunch. Along the wall are the cheesy decorations I saw on my way in. The animatronic ogres. The stuffed unicorn. Waiters dressed up like fantasy characters buzzing from place to place.

A few tables away, I see Gerlaxia. She seems even *less* witchlike now that I've met a real witch. But one thing *hasn't* changed. My owl necklace is still stuck in her wide-brimmed hat.

And I plan to get it back.

I know what you're probably thinking. *Kara, that's the stupidest thing I've ever heard. Did you forget you're being chased by an evil sorceress, a killer oven, and a fire-breathing dragon?*

Yeah, I get it. But that necklace was a gift from my dad. The last thing he ever gave me. It's the whole reason I'm in this mess in the first place. After everything I've been through, it's *right there*. So close. A few feet away.

I'm not about to let it get away again.

I charge toward Gerlaxia. Beneath her pointy purple hat, her eyes suddenly go huge.

"Hey, hold on!" she squeals. "What're you—*hunf!*"

When I grab the owl necklace, the witch's hat snaps off with it.

Beside me, Prince Fred looks totally confused. "You're attacking the wrong witch!"

I untangle my necklace from the witch's hat and shove it into my pocket. That's one problem solved. But I still have lots more to worry about. Like the massive dragon that just landed on a plate of mashed potatoes.

The table collapses beneath the dragon's weight. The creature's leathery wings pound the air. Its sharp teeth glisten.

I spin around, but that route is blocked. At the other end of Legendtopia is the Sorceress. Her dark eyes are fixed on me. Her lips curl into a smile.

All around me, people have stopped eating to watch. And here's the weirdest part: They're smiling. Leaning forward. Excited. They must think this is all part of the show. Even more legendary entertainment from Legendtopia.

And at the edge of the audience is the group I came in with. Mrs. Olyphant is yelling. Other kids are laughing and cheering. Marcy is watching in wide-eyed amazement. At last, her fantasy field trip has gone seriously epic.

As if things aren't bad enough already, now my entire fourth-period class is about to witness my death.

Prince Fred

"Run for your lives!" I scream. "You're all in mortal danger!"

The crowd applauds. Someone at a nearby table yells, "Bravo!"

The dragon unleashes a blast of fire. Groups of diners leap from their tables just in time to avoid being roasted in the flames. I watch as realization slowly settles upon their faces. Their expressions turn from amusement to fear.

People scramble from their wooden benches, spilling food and drinks, racing for the doors.

The walls blaze. Smoke billows across the castle. Voices call out in alarm.

"The restaurant! It's on fire!"

"Everyone out!"

"Run!"

Kara and I stagger through the chaos, past half-eaten plates of food and spilled goblets. Waves of fire and smoke crash all around. Along the way, I glimpse many strange sights. An ogre stands before me, thick arms raised in fury. I flinch, but the creature remains perfectly still. Next I encounter a unicorn. But like the ogre, it doesn't move. Its horn is attached to its head by some form of silver adhesive.

This entire accursed castle is . . .

Fake.

But there is little time to gaze at the peculiarities of my surroundings. Behind me, a wave of people surges for the exit. Kara and I tumble forward, through a doorway, over a minuscule moat (*are those goldfish in the pond beneath me?*), and suddenly . . .

We're outside.

This seems to be some kind of village square. All around the burning castle stand blocky buildings. The signs read FIRST NATIONAL BANK, CRAZY EARL'S ELECTRONICS EXTRAVAGANZA, MCDONALD'S.

I turn to find Kara in the clutches of an older woman.

"You're coming with me," says the woman. "We'll deal with you once we get back to school."

"Mrs. Olyphant, wait!" Kara says. "I was just—"

"Endangering an entire restaurant full of people!" the woman interrupts. "That's what you were doing!"

"Pardon me." I step forward. "Perhaps I might explain."

The woman seems to notice me for the first time. Her brow wrinkles. "Do you go to Shady Pines Middle School?"

"No."

"Then stay out of it!"

I bristle. In my kingdom, speaking to the Royal Prince in such a rude manner would result in any number of horrible punishments. Before I can reply, Mrs. Olyphant snatches Kara by the collar and begins pulling her across the square.

"Wait!" Kara casts an uncertain look back in my direction. "He's with me!"

The woman ignores her pleas. Instead, she drags Kara up the steps of a gargantuan yellow carriage that is lined with many windows.

I watch as everyone heads into the long yellow carriage. It lets out a sound that's disturbingly similar to a troll's mating call. Gray smoke billows out its backside. The door closes and the carriage lurches forward, pulled by a team of unseen horses. Seconds later, it rolls onto the road and drives away.

The one person I know from this world has just vanished.

Kara

The Dungeon smells like moldy textbooks and week-old tacos. A mysterious liquid drips from the ceiling—*plunk, plunk, plunk*—forming a radioactive-looking puddle. The Dungeon is located halfway underground. Grimy windows line the top of the wall, giving a narrow view of the sidewalk outside. I can see the ankles of my classmates strutting past.

After the trouble at Legendtopia, I was given a week in the Dungeon. Which is where kids at Shady Pines Middle are sent for detention.

My pocket vibrates. When I'm sure the Dungeon Guard (aka detention monitor) isn't looking, I remove my phone.

Electronic devices are strictly prohibited in the Dungeon, but my phone's been vibrating nonstop for the past half hour and I can't stand ignoring it any longer. I slide the phone into my lap, where I hope the guard won't see it.

Sixteen new text messages. And they're all from Marcy. I haven't talked to her since my world transformed into a crazy epic fantasy story. After what happened at Legendtopia, we weren't allowed to sit beside each other on the bus. Instead, I had to share a seat with Mrs. Olyphant. As soon as we reached school, I was sent straight to the principal's office. And from there, it was a one-way ticket to the Dungeon.

Hunching over in my desk, I scroll through Marcy's texts.

> OMG! OMG! OMG!
>
> That was EPIC!!!!!!!!
>
> What happened?!?!
>
> What were you doing onstage
>
> And what was up w that dragon?
>
> Definitely not the same puppet we saw first time
>
> It looked REAL
>
> Like REALLY real

And who was that witch lady?

She was freeeeaky!!!!

Way freakier than our waitress

But srsly you gotta tell me

What happened back there

?????

Kara?

Kara?

I stare at the screen until it goes dark. How can I possibly explain any of this to Marcy? How can I explain it to *anyone*?

The events that went down at Legendtopia were insane. The dragon, the Sorceress, the murderous oven.

And Prince Fred.

Last I saw him, he was standing alone in the parking lot, his face smudged with ash, his clothes stained and torn. Right outside Legendtopia, with so many other people decked out in fantasy costumes, the prince didn't look all that out of place. But what if he tried to go somewhere else? I couldn't exactly picture him fitting in with other kids our age. Or people of *any* age, for that matter.

The guy's from another world.

Literally.

And it isn't like he can go back to his kingdom. Not while Legendtopia is occupied by the Sorceress.

He's stuck here.

I remind myself it isn't my fault. He *wanted* to come. I never volunteered to babysit a fairy-tale prince.

But still—I can't help it. I feel sorry for him. He saved my life back there. And now he's all alone. Stranded in a strange new world.

Prince Fred

What a magnificent new world!

Standing outside Legendtopia, I marvel at my surroundings. My skin tingles with bewilderment, amazement, bafflement, and awe.

Everything is new and wondrous!

On the other side of the square, carriages made of steel are pulled by invisible horses. They move at dazzling speeds, carrying bored-looking people from one place to another.

Everyone seems to own the same glowing device that Kara used inside the walk-in refrigerator. My mind grasps for the word. *Self-Own.* That's it. Not only can this

Self-Own be used for creating light in the darkness, some people also lift it to their ears and speak to it!

"Hey, it's me," a nearby woman says to her Self-Own. "You would not *believe* what just happened. You know that place Legendtopia? The tacky fake-castle restaurant? It caught on fire!"

The woman goes silent. Gripping the Self-Own to her ear, she nods several times, muttering "Uh-huh," and "Exactly."

I narrow my eyes, trying to make sense of what I'm seeing. There's only one explanation.

The Self-Own is whispering into her ear!

But what is it saying? What secrets does the Self-Own possess?

Many others seek counsel from their own Self-Owns. Some stare into the apparatus blankly. Others jab it repeatedly with their thumbs. Probably as punishment for unwise advice.

Soon enough, the crowd outside Legendtopia has cleared and the square fills with many fantastical horseless carriages. Each is topped with magical lights that flash red and blue. Some are boxy and white. Others are blue. Two of them are long and red, covered with ladders and hoses.

Several men emerge from the long red carriage. They're wearing the strangest armor I have ever seen. Black-and-yellow coats, with matching pants and helmets. One of the men grips an ax. Two more grab a hose. As a group, they charge toward the flaming building.

There can be only one explanation. The men are soldiers. And they are storming the castle.

It's sure to be an epic battle. And I'm not about to miss it.

Which is why I follow the soldiers.

The square is pure pandemonium. Magical flashing carriages, a flaming castle, strangely dressed soldiers.

Nobody notices me.

I race around the side of Legendtopia. Crouching between a couple of tall hedges, I peer through a window. Nearly everyone has vacated Legendtopia. The castle only has one occupant now.

The Sorceress.

She stands on the charred stage, examining her new castle. The walls are burned, the curtains tattered and ruined. Tables and chairs are littered with spilled food and drinks. Smoke hangs in the air. Ashes drift like snowflakes.

Her attention is drawn to the door. A great crashing

noise erupts and the door shatters. An instant later, the first soldier enters, an ax gripped in his hands. He is followed by the hose-wielding soldiers.

I inch closer to the window, eager to see the Sorceress defeated by the magical soldiers of Urth.

Except that's not what happens. Not even close.

Within seconds, I realize—the soldiers aren't here to fight the Sorceress. They're here to fight the *fire*.

But they don't get very far. With the flick of a wrist, the Sorceress casts an enchantment spell. That's all it takes to stop the soldiers. Their faces go slack. A dull nothingness fills their eyes. They turn and stumble back the way they came.

They're no longer themselves. They've fallen under the Sorceress's control. Their voices call out to the others in the square.

"Fire's contained, guys! It's all under control! Everyone clear out!"

Within an hour, the crowd has dispersed. As the fire dies away, the peculiar flashing carriages depart from the square. Nobody remains outside Legendtopia.

Except me.

And there's nobody inside.

Except the Sorceress.

But what can I do? Alone and without any weaponry, I don't stand a chance against a powerful witch.

And so I watch.

I watch as the Sorceress makes Legendtopia her own.

She starts by replacing the door. Summoning the magic that flows in her veins, she reaches out one pale hand. White light streaks from her fingers. Thick steel planks take shape before her eyes. Their pieces join together like a jigsaw puzzle. Merging. Many pieces becoming one. And from the ground arises a new door.

But the Sorceress doesn't stop there.

Next she focuses her magic on the walls. The flimsy, fake stones begin to quiver and shake. Hardening, strengthening. Solidifying into real stone.

The Sorceress concentrates.

Magic pulses all around her.

She turns her attention to the rows of tables. Casting her spell causes the tables to descend. Deeper and deeper. As if the floor is made of sinking sand.

Plates slide off tables. Goblets tumble sideways. The mess is swallowed into the floor. Gone.

It's a slow process. Little by little. Bit by bit. But gradually . . .

Legendtopia.

Is.

Changing.

I clench my hands into fists, hardly able to fathom what I'm witnessing.

A new pillar grows up from the floor like a tree. Stone turrets branch from the sides of the castle, stretching far into the sky.

The Sorceress pauses. She glances around the room. I duck, but it isn't me that she notices. It's an entirely different audience. All the objects she enchanted—they've come to watch her work. The dragon, the fairies. Even the oven has clattered into the Great Hall.

"It's time to make you some friends!" the Sorceress announces.

At the edge of the room is the stuffed ogre I saw earlier. In my world, ogres are hulking creatures. Dull-witted, frightening, stinky. This ogre only looks stinky. Loose bits of cotton poke through torn stitching. It's wearing a shirt that reads I HAD A LEGENDARY TIME AT LEGENDTOPIA. There's nothing intimidating about any of this.

Until the Sorceress works her magic.

A blast of light from her pale fingers, and the ogre begins to grow. Its small black eyes flick from side to side. Its jaws open. Inside are thick teeth that definitely aren't made of cotton. With a thudding footstep, the ogre steps out of its case.

I read the Sorceress's lips as she speaks to her minion. "Welcome to Legendtopia," she says.

"THANK YOU, MISSUS SORCERESS," it responds in a loud, grunting voice that shakes the windowpane.

I watch in fearful awe as she tours her castle, adding more minions along the way. Suits of armor. A cheese-stained unicorn. A half-dozen ogres.

Her very own army.

I stagger away from the window. I can't allow the Sorceress to wreak havoc on Urth. I must stop her. But how? If I tell the truth, everyone will think I've lost my mind.

Well, almost everyone.

There is still *one* person I can talk to. I just need to find her.

I climb out of the bushes and sneak around the other side of Legendtopia. There I meet a road. Checking carefully to make sure there aren't any horseless carriages around, I stagger to the other side. Another square, filled with unmoving steel carriages. Surrounded by more peculiar buildings.

In front of me, a woman is loading brown paper satchels

from a wheeled cart into the back of her steel carriage. And in one hand, she's gripping a Self-Own.

As I approach the woman, I remind myself that I'm in a different world now. *Act natural,* I think. *Like any other twelve-year-old boy.*

"Pardon me, madam," I begin. "May I seek counsel with your Self-Own?"

The woman stares at me for a long moment. "Uh . . . okay. Here you go."

She hands me the Self-Own. The device is lighter than I expected. Its surface is smooth and shiny. Tentatively, I lift it to my ear, as I've seen others do.

Then I hesitate.

What am I supposed to say? As far as I can tell, the Self-Own does whatever people ask it to do. It answers questions, gives advice, offers help. All the tasks of a servant. A small, shiny servant. And fortunately for me, I have lots of experience ordering servants around.

"Fetch me a carriage," I say to the Self-Own in a commanding voice. "Or a horse will do. But not an invisible one. And I am growing rather hungry. Bring me a meal of roasted pheasant."

With the Self-Own pressed against my ear, I wait for the apparatus to whisper its response. Nothing happens. I wait a moment longer. Still nothing.

Meanwhile, the woman is staring at me with her mouth hanging open.

Perhaps the Self-Own needs punishment. Doing my best to mimic the others I've observed, I bang my thumbs against the device.

"Do not ignore me, insolent devil! I demand that you—"

The woman snatches the Self-Own out of my hand. "Uh ... maybe I can help. My name's Debra. What's yours?"

"My name is Frederick Alexander Siegfried Maria Thorston the Fourteenth, Prince of Heldstone." I bow.

The woman glances across the street at Legendtopia. "I'm guessing you just came from that castle restaurant?"

"Precisely."

"Well, you definitely won't be going back to work today. Not after the fire. How're you getting home? Should I call your parents—"

"No!" My response comes too quickly, and too loudly. I adjust my tone. "I mean, my mother and father aren't available. Not at the moment. But perhaps I could ride with you?"

"Uh ..." Debra casts an uncertain glance at her Self-Own. "You sure there isn't anyone else I can call?"

"Positive."

Debra hesitates a moment longer. "Fine. Where do you need to go?"

I remember something Mrs. Olyphant said earlier. *Shady Pines Middle School.* That's where Kara Estrada must be.

I adjust my ash-covered waistcoat. "Take me to Shady Pines Middle School."

Kara

———

After an hour in the Dungeon, the September sunshine hits me like a spotlight. I shield my face. My eyes are still adjusting to the brightness when a dark blob appears in front of me. I blink twice and realize the blob is Prince Fred.

"Greetings, Kara Estrada!"

I rub my eyes. This has to be some kind of post-detention hallucination. But when I look again, Prince Fred's still there.

"How'd you *get* here?" I ask.

"A kindly woman gave me a ride in her carriage," the prince explains. "Did you know that carriages here aren't pulled by invisible horses? They're propelled by something called crasopline."

"You mean *gasoline?*"

"That's the word! *Gasoline!* It's quite a marvelous technology, don't you agree?"

I shrug. "I've never really thought about it before."

"Your world is *full of* fantastical wonders. Such as the boxes that hang above streets with shifting colors of illumination inside them. Depending upon the color, drivers know whether to stop or go—"

"Traffic lights?"

"Yes, exactly! They're spectacular! But sadly, I didn't come here to discuss gasoline and traffic lights. I bring with me disturbing news."

"What?"

A grim look passes over Prince Fred's face. "Legendtopia has been overtaken by the Sorceress. And she has made some . . . changes."

"What kind of changes?"

The prince takes a deep breath. Then he begins describing how the Sorceress worked her dark magic on Legendtopia, turning it into her own personal fortress and transforming lifeless objects into her minions.

"But why Legendtopia?" I ask. "It's just a restaurant. What does she want with it?"

"Legendtopia is only the beginning." Prince Fred shudders. "I fear the Sorceress has much more planned for your world."

"Like *what?*"

Before he can explain anything else, Trevor Fitzgerald interrupts our conversation. I haven't spoken to him since he was teasing Marcy at Legendtopia.

"Hey, Kara." His attention turns to the prince. "Who's your friend?"

"None of your business," I snap.

Trevor gawks at Prince Fred like he's ... well, from another world. He lets out a mocking chuckle. "Nice clothes."

I guess they don't have sarcasm where Fred comes from, because he takes the insult as a compliment. Bowing, he says, "Many thanks!"

"Go bother someone else, Trevor," I say.

He saunters away, snickering to himself. I turn my focus back to Prince Fred.

"We need to get you some normal clothes," I say.

An offended look crosses his face. "What do you mean? My clothes are the finest in the kingdom."

"Maybe in *your* kingdom. But here, nobody wears stuff like that. If you're gonna hang out in my world, then you can't draw so much attention to yourself."

He gives this some thought. "Where do you suggest I obtain this new clothing?"

I hesitate. And even before I speak, I know it's a bad idea.

"Come on," I say finally. "Let's go to my house."

———

The walk home from school normally takes ten minutes. With Prince Fred, it's closer to an hour.

I swear, the guy can't go more than five feet without stopping to gush over another "amazing" new thing he's just noticed. A glob of chewed gum on the sidewalk, a bicycle chained to a fence, a stop sign. According to Prince Fred, they're "stupendous," "magnificent," "wonderful" (in that order).

You should see what a big deal he makes when he sees a fire hydrant. He circles the thing from a safe distance.

"Fascinating," he whispers. "So this contraption creates fire?"

I roll my eyes. "It doesn't create fire. It shoots water out of that big nozzle."

"Then why don't they call it a *water* hydrant?"

"I don't know."

A minivan drives past. Kids in the back turn in their

seats to stare at Prince Fred as they go by. A few seconds later, a teenager on a bike rides past. Pointing at Prince Fred, he calls out, "Lookin' good, dork!"

"Many thanks!" the prince calls back.

The teenager rides on, laughing so hard he nearly runs into a telephone pole.

"What is a dork?" Prince Fred asks.

I grit my teeth. "Let's just go."

Soon we reach the entrance to Pevensie Park. I always cut through the park on my way home. It's no big deal, really. Just a dirt path through some tall trees. Of course, the prince doesn't see it that way.

"Do you have fairies in this forest?" he asks.

"No."

"Ogres?"

"Nope."

"Unicorns?"

I stop walking and turn to Prince Fred. "None of those things exists in this world."

The prince's forehead wrinkles. "But of course they do. I saw all of them in Legendtopia."

"Those are fake."

"I know, but . . . why would anyone create fake creatures when the real ones don't exist?"

"I guess they like to pretend. And by the way, this isn't some kind of forest. It's just a little park. Nothing special."

But the prince isn't paying attention to me. He's focused on a frog that just hopped onto the path.

Fred moves slowly toward the frog. "Greetings, forest creature. Tell me, how do you like the Kingdom of Shady Pines?"

The frog sits there, because that's what frogs do. Prince Fred waits politely, like he's actually expecting a response.

Finally, I speak up. "You know it can't understand you, right? It's a frog. Frogs don't talk."

The prince looks from the frog to me. "They don't?"

I shake my head.

"So then, which creatures *do* speak?" he asks.

"None of them. Animals don't talk here. Well, except maybe parrots. But they don't really count."

Prince Fred lets out a disbelieving laugh. "What a strange world you inhabit."

"I could say the same for you," I mutter.

I lead the prince into a clearing, past a playground and back onto the path. On the other side of the park is my street. I try to hurry Fred along, but he's way too interested in all the "marvelous sights" (in other words, mailboxes and recycling bins).

When we finally reach my house, I take us through the door that leads into the laundry room. While Prince Fred examines the washing machine, I nudge the dining room door open and peer inside. The coast is clear. Which is a good thing, since I'm really not in the mood to explain to anyone in my family what I'm doing hanging out with a prince from another world.

We're halfway across the dining room when I hear footsteps. I freeze. Prince Fred opens his mouth to speak, but I shush him.

"You need to hide!" I whisper.

The prince gives me a confused look. "Hide? Why do I need to—"

"Just do it! Quick!"

The footsteps are getting closer. I jump forward, swing open the door to the pantry, and shove Prince Fred inside. The moment I slam the door shut, my mom enters the dining room. She must've just returned from a shift at the hospital. She's still wearing her blue nurse's uniform and name badge.

"Hi, Kara. I didn't hear you—" Mom goes silent when she notices my clothes. My shirt's torn and charred from the fire. Ashes stain my jeans. "What happened? Are you okay?"

"I'm fine. Really."

Mom shakes her head. She's obviously waiting for further explanation. I know I'll have to tell her about the trouble I got in at school eventually. But that conversation will have to wait until I'm *not* hiding a prince in the pantry.

Fortunately, right at that moment, a distraction comes along. *Un*fortunately, the distraction is my little brother, Neal.

"Hey, booger brains!" he squeals at me.

"Shut up, slug face!" I say.

"Kids!" Mom warns. "Language."

"I'm hungry!" Neal skips a circle around our mom, waving his arms. "Can I have a snack?"

Neal's nine years old. He's also the most annoying person on earth. Imagine a tornado with a chili-bowl haircut.

"Snack! Snack! Snack!" he chants. "I want a snack!"

"All right, all right." Mom rolls her eyes. "There are crackers in the pantry."

Neal makes a move for the pantry, but I quickly step in his way. "You know what—I'll get those for you."

Mom narrows her eyes at me. "What's going on?"

"Nothing." My voice squeaks. "Can't I do something nice for my little bro?"

"That would be the first time in the history of the world," Neal points out. He wriggles to get past me.

"I do nice stuff for you all the time!" I say as I shove Neal.

"Ow!" he squeals. "Kara pushed me!"

Mom crosses her arms. "Kara, is there something you want to tell me?"

"No, I just—"

Neal bolts past before I can stop him. The door to the pantry swings open and I hear my brother gasp.

"Mooo-oooom!" he screams. "Kara's hiding a pirate in the pantry!"

Prince Fred

I'll admit that my clothing is a little ragged. My hair's out of place and my face is stained with ashes. I'm not my usual well-groomed self.

But a pirate? How rude!

The little boy who intruded on my hiding spot turns out to be Kara's brother. Like his sister, the boy has dark hair and brown eyes.

And standing behind him is a pretty woman with olive-colored skin. Kara's mother.

Because all three appear too bewildered at my presence to speak a word, I figure I might as well introduce myself.

"Greetings!" I bow to Kara's mother and give a curt nod

to her brother. "I apologize for my unannounced visit. My name is—"

"Fred!" Kara interrupts. "His name's Fred."

I'm not particularly fond of this new name, but I'm in Kara's home. And her world. She knows more about the customs of this place. And so I grit my teeth and fake a smile.

"That is correct," I say. "My name is Fred."

Kara's mother reaches out to shake my hand. "It's a pleasure to meet you, Fred. I'm Mrs. Estrada. And this is Kneel."

In my world, *kneel* is a thing people do when I walk by. Apparently, here it's a name.

"Where are you from?" Kneel asks.

"I come from a faraway—"

"England!" Kara blurts out. "He's an exchange student. From England."

Mrs. Estrada gives me a closer look. "So that explains the accent."

Kneel tugs at my waistcoat. "Does *everyone* dress so weird in England?"

I turn a confused glance in Kara's direction. We didn't discuss any of this. I don't even know what England *is*.

Kara gives me a tiny shrug, as if to say, *What choice do*

we have? Then she turns back to her mom. "Fred just arrived in Shady Pines. On a student exchange program. He was supposed to be staying with this other family. But the kid . . . uh—got sick."

"That's unfortunate," Mrs. Estrada replies. "What kind of illness?"

Kara hesitates. I can see her brain spinning. And so I offer a reply—at the same moment that she does.

"Measles," I say.

"Pinkeye," she says.

Mrs. Estrada's forehead wrinkles. "The kid came down with measles . . . *and* pinkeye . . . at the same time?"

Kara and I both nod.

"Sounds itchy," observes Kneel.

"So—uh . . . obviously Fred can't stay with this other kid," Kara continues. "At least, not right now. But since he's already here, he needs to live *somewhere.* So today at school, I sort of . . . volunteered our house. Just temporarily, of course."

Mrs. Estrada folds her arms. Her eyes flick back and forth between Kara and me. A nervous buzz rattles the inside of my skull. What if Kara's mother sees through our deception? What if she kicks me out? Where will I go?

But then a smile creeps across Mrs. Estrada's face. "Of course you can stay here, Fred."

I exhale a grateful breath. But the wave of relief is instantly washed away by what Mrs. Estrada says next.

"You can sleep in Kneel's room."

"Yay!" Kara's little brother gives my coat several more sharp yanks. "Me and the pirate are gonna be roomies!"

Kara

———

Now I *really* feel sorry for Prince Fred. He's gotten himself stuck in another world, chased by an evil witch, and nearly burned to a crisp by a giant dragon. But that's nothing compared to what he's about to face:

Sharing a room with my little brother.

"Here it is!" Neal pushes open the door to his bedroom.

Prince Fred stumbles to a halt. He scans the piles of dirty laundry on the bed, the crayon markings on the wall, the game controllers spilled across the floor.

"What happened to your bedchamber?" he says to Neal. "Did your servants forget to clean it?"

"Servants? We don't have any servants."

"I can tell." Prince Fred sniffs and makes a face. "And where shall I be residing?"

"Right here." Neal points to the floor. "My mom's setting up an air mattress."

Prince Fred frowns. "Well, it's certainly . . . *cozy.*"

The prince might've found a place to stay, but he still needs some new clothes. Since all of Neal's things are too small, that leaves him with only one choice. I lead him into my room and open the dresser.

"You're gonna have to borrow some of my clothes," I say.

Prince Fred huffs in disbelief. "First you cram me into a tiny, foul-smelling bedchamber with your brother. And now you expect me to wear *your* drab, unsightly clothing? This must be a cruel joke!"

I glance at the open doorway to make sure my mom and brother aren't listening in. Lowering my voice, I whisper, "Don't forget—*you* followed *me* through that walk-in refrigerator. I'm doing you a favor here. So don't go around talking smack about my clothes. Got it?"

Prince Fred sighs. "I apologize. I don't mean to be a rude houseguest. This is all just such a tremendous change for me. Thank you for sharing your hideous clothing with me."

It's not exactly the nicest apology in the world, but at least it's something.

"For as long as you're here, you'll have to go to school," I say. "Otherwise, people will get suspicious. We can try to enroll you tomorrow. And you'll need a backpack. I think there's one in here somewhere."

I open my closet, searching through clothes and old stuffed animals. In the back corner, the edge of a shoe box pokes out from beneath a pile of laundry. Faded, worn at the sides from being opened and sorted through a million times.

Before Fred notices it, I nudge the box out of sight.

Then I find what I'm looking for. My old backpack. I stopped using it in the second grade. It's bright purple, covered with sparkles, and decorated with cartoon unicorns. Most guys wouldn't be caught dead wearing such a girly backpack, but Fred actually looks excited to try it on.

"At last! Something with style!" His eyes land on the sparkles. "And it's festooned with such interesting jewels."

"Oh." Surprise fills my voice. "I thought you might want to trade, but—"

"That won't be necessary." Fred struts in front of the mirror, admiring the backpack. "I shall wear it with pride."

While he's busy examining cartoon unicorns and sparkles, I dig out a few T-shirts and socks. I know my jeans aren't big enough to fit him, but luckily I have some sweat-pants with an elastic waist. They're bright green with stripes down the sides.

I press the clothes into his hands. Prince Fred just stares at them.

"What's wrong?" I ask.

"It's just ..." He pauses. "Usually, my servants dress me."

My jaw might've just fallen to the ground. "Don't even *think* about asking me to help you with *that*."

"Very well." He hesitates. "Now what?"

"Um ... you're pretty dirty from the fire. Before you change, you might wanna shower off."

By the blank stare the prince gives me, I'm guessing they don't have showers in his kingdom, either. I lead him into the bathroom that I share with Neal.

Once again, the prince is clueless.

This is definitely not the way I expected to spend my afternoon. Giving a prince from another world a step-by-step tutorial in Bathroom Basics 101. But what choice do I have? It's not like we can check the guy into a Holiday Inn for the night.

—

I leave the prince alone to do his thing. Back in my bedroom, I open the closet door. Pushing aside some laundry, I reach into the back corner of the closet and remove the shoe box.

Settling onto the floor, I pull the top off the box. Inside is a collection of papers and trinkets. A faded plane ticket from over twenty years ago. A broken calculator watch. A half-empty bottle of cologne.

To most people, the things inside the box would probably look like random junk. But to me, they're memories.

Memories of my dad.

The plane ticket is for a flight from Buenos Aires to Los Angeles. The first time Dad ever came to the United States. The calculator watch is the one he wore for years, until the digital numbers faded and the calculations came out all wrong (2 + 2 = 17). The cologne came from Dad's side of the medicine cabinet in my parents' bathroom. The one he wore on special occasions.

After Dad disappeared, I went through the house, collecting his things. I was like a detective looking for evidence. There had to be a clue somewhere. A hint. Anything that could tell me *why*.

Why did he leave us? Why didn't he tell us where he was going? Why has he never written or called?

Why?

But the weeks turned into months, and the months turned into years. And Dad never came back. Somewhere along the way, I realized, the shoe box wasn't going to help me find him. But it still helped me remember him. Now I pull it out at times when I feel alone and scared. When the world gets too big, too crazy, too *whatever*.

Times like this.

The doorway to another world, the witch assembling her evil army, the prince using my shower. Things can't possibly get any crazier. And it's not like I can tell Mom or Neal about it. I can't call a friend or post about it on Facebook.

So instead, I plop down in front of the shoe box. I reach into my pocket and run a thumb over the owl necklace. Closing my eyes, I imagine that Dad's here right now.

What would he do in a situation like this?

I'm still puzzling over this question when I hear footsteps headed in the direction of my room. I slide the box into the corner of my closet. In the next moment, Fred appears in the doorway. His shirt's inside out and his sweatpants are backward. Around his neck, he's wearing his towel like a cape.

"Look!" He grins proudly. "I got dressed all by myself!"

Prince Fred

Returning to Kneel's bedchamber, I stand in the doorway, dumbfounded by my new surroundings. The place is horribly messy. It smells like it's inhabited by an ogre with digestive problems. And yet . . . it is filled with all kinds of remarkable and exotic objects. Something called a "laptop" grants access to an enchanted portal known as "the Internet." Through this portal, people can obtain all the knowledge of all the libraries on Urth. Although in Kneel's case, he mostly uses it to rewatch a "YouTube video" of a cat getting its head stuck in a pickle jar.

He has an incredible box of endless entertainment known as "video games." He carries thousands of songs in his pocket and can listen to any of them whenever he wants.

Kara says that there's no magic on Urth, but from what I have seen, there's magic everywhere.

When it comes time for dinner, I join Kara's family at the dining room table. But instead of our food being served on silver platters, like in my palace, dinner arrives in two flat boxes.

They call it "pizza."

Despite my growling stomach, I'm hesitant to try it. Honestly—what kind of food comes in a box? Kara's family doesn't even use silverware. Instead, they devour their pizza with their hands. Like common trolls.

But I'm a visitor in this new world. And so I cautiously take a bite. And another. And another. Soon I'm eagerly stuffing my mouth.

I slam a fist on the table. "I declare pizza to be the most delicious cuisine in the world!"

Kara's family looks at me like I've lost my mind. I reach for another piece.

After dinner, Kara introduces me to yet another new discovery. Toothpaste. In Heldstone, we brush our teeth with herbs that have been crushed into powder by dwarfs. Here the paste simply squirts out of a tube.

We stand together in the small bathroom as I brush back and forth. The toothpaste drips down my chin.

"Dissus kite dayddy," I say.

Kara squints at me in the mirror. "What?"

I spit, then repeat myself. "This is quite tasty."

"If you say so."

While I brush, Kara reaches into her pocket and removes a necklace. The same necklace she was determined to rescue at Legendtopia. A memory springs to mind: Kara attacking a witch, snatching the silver owl from the witch's pointy hat.

The silver owl twirls and dangles in the light.

I point at it with my toothbrush. "Rurrey rreggluss."

"What?" Kara asks.

I spit another glob of toothpaste. "I said, 'Lovely necklace.'"

"Thanks." She holds the silver chain in front of her. "My dad gave it to me."

"Your dad? Is he . . . ?" I hesitate, unsure how to phrase the question. "I mean, did he—"

"He's not around," Kara says.

"What happened?"

All the air seems to leave the room. I watch Kara's reflection in the mirror. She watches the floor.

"The day after he gave me the necklace, my dad just . . . left." In the reflection, Kara's brown eyes search the bathroom floor, as if the memory is printed there. "This was three years ago. He went to work one day and never came back. We haven't heard from him since."

"Perhaps something happened to him," I suggest. "Perhaps he didn't intend to leave for such a long time."

Kara shakes her head. "He packed his suitcase. He planned it all out ahead of time. And never told anyone. Just snuck away one day. Since then, he hasn't contacted any of us. No phone calls, no letters. Not even an email."

I have no idea what an "email" is, but I sense that this isn't the right time to ask.

Kara continues: "My dad moved here from Argentina. That's another country, far away from here. Back in Argentina, he was an electrical engineer. But he couldn't work the same kind of job in America. He didn't have the right degrees. People thought his English wasn't good enough. Mom says that must be why he left. To move back to Argentina. She figures he was sick of people assuming he wasn't smart because of his accent. Instead of an engineer, he was stuck working as an electrician—"

The toothbrush drops from my mouth. "An electrician?"

"Yeah. People would, like, call him if their electricity wasn't working. Or if they needed something rewired."

A memory stirs in my brain as I mutter the strange syllables under my breath. "E-lec-trish-ian."

By this point, Kara's giving me an extremely odd look. "Uh . . . why do you care so much about my dad's job?"

"I have something to show you." My voice quavers. "Something that might be very important."

A glob of toothpaste hangs from my chin, but I have more important things to think about now. I rush out of the bathroom.

Kara calls after me, "Would you mind explaining what's going on?"

I don't reply. Instead, I hurry into Kneel's room. Kara follows.

By the time she steps into the messy room, I'm digging through the pockets of my old clothing.

"Seal the door!" I say in a frantic voice. "We can't risk your brother overhearing us."

"He's watching TV with my mom," Kara replies. But she closes the door anyway. "Are you gonna tell me what's going on or not?"

Rather than an answer, I let out an excited gasp. In the pocket of my waistcoat, I find what I'm looking for.

The scrap of parchment.

"What's that?" Kara asks.

I tell her about the poem. How it was intercepted by my father's spies. How I found the Royal Tutor studying its meaning. And how I stole it from the old geezer.

Kara looks back at me like I'm speaking Elvish. "Great story. But what does any of that have to do with my dad?"

I hold up the scrap. "This poem may tell us what happened to your father."

Kara

⌒

"What does a poem from another world have to do with my dad?"

The prince shakes his head. "I don't know exactly. I hid it in my pocket. But with all the excitement, I forgot all about it. Until you mentioned that your father was an electrician—"

"So?"

"This poem mentions a similar word." The prince scans the tattered scrap until he finds what he's looking for. He begins to read aloud: " 'People flocked, far and wide, to listen to the fantastical tales of the Elektro-Magician.' " He looks up at me with wide-eyed excitement. "Do you see now? What if there's a connection? What if this poem contains a clue about your father's disappearance?"

"But my dad isn't an Elektro . . ." I stumble over the word. "Elektro-Magician."

"Perhaps not in your world. But if he visited Heldstone? If he stumbled through the miniature door, like you—"

"Just stop it!"

My voice comes out louder than I'd expected. Fred suddenly goes quiet. He stares at me, confused. For a long moment, the only sound comes from the living room. The muffled rumble of the TV.

"Please," I say in a croaked whisper. "Please—just stop talking about my dad like . . . like . . ."

I can't get the words past the lump in my throat. Instead, they echo inside my head.

Stop talking about my dad like he's still around.

Three years ago, when my dad first disappeared, I was sure he would return. *Any day now,* I thought. Repeating the words to myself again and again, as if they could bring him back.

Any day now, he'll step through the door. *Any day now,* I'll hear the sound of his heavy boots clomping next to the washing machine. *Any day now,* his voice will call out to us in his accent that turns every sentence into music. *Any day now,* I'll run to meet him. *Any day now,* he'll wrap his strong arms around me, and I'll smell the mixture of oil and charred wires that always clings to his clothes after work.

Any day now.

But the days kept going by, and Dad didn't come home.

Until finally, I stopped repeating the words. I stopped expecting his return. It hurt too much.

I drop onto Neal's bed, my vision blurring with tears. I try to blink them away. I'm not going to cry. Not now. Not in front of Prince Fred.

The mattress sags. Prince Fred sits beside me. Through the tears, I can tell he's holding the scrap of parchment in one hand. His other hand comes to rest on my shoulder.

"I'm sorry about your father," he says. "But perhaps this message can tell you what happened to him. Perhaps if we read the poem in its entirety . . ."

I let out an exasperated breath. Over the past three years, not a single day has gone by that I haven't wondered what happened to my dad. I collected the things he left behind. I searched the Internet. I wrote to relatives. Not a clue. I seriously doubt that some stupid poem from another world is going to help.

But if it'll get Fred to leave me alone, then fine . . . whatever. Let's have a poetry reading.

"All right." I sigh. "Show me the poem."

Prince Fred carefully holds the piece of parchment between us. The poem is written in a smooth, looping script.

From a distant, unknown land came he.
A Traveler he claimed to be.
People flocked, far and wide, to listen
To the fantastical tales of the Elektro-Magician.
With him, he carried a box of enchantment
Bringing great wonders to our remote encampment.
His tools filled darkness with illumination:
Flames and sparks and marvelous flotation.
So beloved was the Traveler to our clan
That we clasped heavy chains around the man.
And now we take him with us everywhere we go
To charge a handsome fee for his marvelous show.

As I read the poem, a shaky unease comes over me. My first thought is *This has to be some kind of practical joke. A trick.* Except I know Prince Fred wouldn't do something like that. This poem came from his world. And there are details in there. Details only my family knows about.

When I glance up at the prince again, he's staring at me. His blue eyes are filled with expectation.

"This is . . ." I hesitate. The words feel thick in my mouth. "This is incredible."

Fred grips the parchment a little tighter. "So you think perhaps this poem refers to . . . to—"

"My dad? Yes."

"What makes you so certain?"

"Lots of things. I mean, look at the first line." I point at the beginning of the poem and read the line out loud. "*From a distant, unknown land came he.*' That could be here. Earth. And the part about him being an . . . an Elektro-Magician. He's not a magician, but sometimes he would put on little shows for me and my brother. And it was *like magic*. He would get out his toolbox—"

"'That could be his '*box of enchantment*'!" the prince says excitedly.

"Exactly! Then there're these two lines." My finger moves down the rough paper. I read the lines in a shaky whisper. "'*His tools filled darkness with illumination, / Flames and sparks and marvelous flotation.*' That's exactly the kind of thing he used to do with me and Neal. He'd, like, use wires and circuits to create mini-fireworks shows. Or he'd make magnets float."

I try to keep my breathing steady. Just when I'd given up hope of finding my dad, he suddenly pops up again—in a poem from another world. But if the "Elektro-Magician" really *is* my dad, how'd he end up in Heldstone? The prince says there's only one entrance to his world. The miniature door. And if that's the case, then maybe, just maybe . . .

I jump up from Neal's bed. Prince Fred looks confused. But I'm already bolting into the hallway. He stumbles after me, bringing the parchment with him. In my room, I throw open my closet and kick aside a pile of dirty laundry until I find what I'm looking for.

The shoe box.

Prince Fred

The box is full of trinkets and clutter.

"What are these things?" I ask.

"My dad's old stuff." Kara removes a booklet. Slips of yellow and white paper covered in handwritten scribbles. "These are work orders. My dad filled one out for every job he did. After he disappeared, I stashed this away. I've looked through it like a million times. But I never knew what I was looking for. Until now."

Kara flips through the booklet. The dates written on each slip are chronological. She thumbs forward in time until the last work order with any of her father's handwriting.

"This." She points at the date. "It's two days before he went missing."

Her finger slides to the next line of handwriting, where her father scribbled a single word:

LEGENDTOPIA

Beneath that is another line of handwriting:

WALK-IN REFRIGERATOR BROKEN

The booklet shakes in Kara's hands. "My dad—he went to Legendtopia two days before he disappeared."

"It cannot be a coincidence." I stare at the work order, my thoughts spinning. "He visited Legendtopia to inspect the broken walk-in refrigerator. And while there—that's when he discovered the doorway—"

"He must've known he'd stumbled onto something incredible," Kara says. "Another world. And I'm guessing he wanted to go back. To see it again. He's an adventurous guy. He'd already moved to another continent. Started a whole new life. Why not explore another world?"

Kara's eyes widen. She pulls the owl necklace from her pocket.

"Dad couldn't tell me the truth. I would've never believed him. So he gave me this." She holds up the silver necklace. "His way of saying goodbye. In case he never came back."

"So your father went through the doorway the first time," I say, stitching together the time line. "Then he came home. He packed his bag. Which means he must've been planning a longer trip the next time. And he never came back because . . ."

My eyes fall back onto the parchment. A chilled silence blankets the room as I read the final four lines again.

"Because he's still in Heldstone," I say. "He's being held captive."

"Captive?" Kara's voice comes out as a hoarse croak. "How? Who did this?"

"The Royal Tutor says that the message was being passed among the Thurphenwald tribe. A nomadic civilization. Known for their traveling carnival shows and poor grooming habits."

"So you're saying this Thurphen-*whatever* tribe—they captured my dad?"

I nod. "And it appears as if they've been using him as one of their traveling attractions."

For years, Kara assumed her father abandoned her. But this is even worse.

He's a prisoner in another world.

I wake up the next morning to a disturbing sight: a grubby, smelly, screaming nine-year-old boy with hair poking up in all directions.

"Rise and shine, roomie!" Kneel's voice rattles my brain. "Wake up! Wake up!"

The circumstances of my new life gradually come back to me. It's my first morning in this new world. Urth. And I just woke up in the bedchamber of Kara's younger brother.

"Will you please stop yelling?" I groan.

"But it's time to get up! You're late for your first day of school!"

I pull on the borrowed pair of green sweatpantaloons and the tea-shirt. In the dining room, I find Kara alone at the table next to a silver device. It takes me a moment to remember its name. A laptop.

Kara points at the apparatus. "Check this out."

Hunching over the laptop, I begin to read.

FIRE AT "LEGENDARY" RESTAURANT

The crowd at the fantasy-theme restaurant Legendtopia was served a dish of terrifying with a side of freaky on Tuesday afternoon when a fire forced the building to be evacuated.

Witnesses claim that the culprits are two middle-school children who escaped from their field trip and caused mayhem—sneaking into the kitchen, interrupting the usual lunchtime performance, and hijacking a dragon puppet. When the puppet's built-in flame dispenser went out of control, a fire quickly spread, sending patrons rushing for the exits.

"Those kids were reckless!" said Lydia Gelding, whose business lunch was interrupted by chaos. "One of them tackled a witch. The other was wielding that puppet like a flamethrower. It's a miracle nobody got hurt."

Legendtopia will be closed until further notice. Due to health risks, other stores in the shopping center announced that they would be closing as well.

"This laptop is full of lies!" I slam my fist on the table. "That dragon was *real!*"

"Keep your voice down!" Kara glances over her shoulder to make sure we're alone. "It says they're closing other stores in the shopping center. Do you think the Sorceress is behind it?"

I nod. "I'm certain of it. I saw the way she enchanted the firesoldiers—"

"Fire*fighters*."

"Whatever! The Sorceress influences people. She makes them do her bidding. She probably enchanted the other merchants as well."

"She's already taken over Legendtopia. Now it's the entire shopping center."

"And with the army she's building?" I say slowly. "This is only the beginning."

Kara

Before leaving for school, there's one more thing I have to do.

"I'll meet you outside in a sec," I say to Fred. "I need to say goodbye."

Once the door closes behind Fred, I turn to my mom. Light from the window swims in her eyes. A minute earlier, my mission had seemed so clear. Return to Heldstone. Find Dad. Bring him back.

Now I'm not so sure. What if I don't return? What if I never see Mom or Neal again? And the worst part is, I can't even tell them the truth. They'd never believe me. Or worse—Mom wouldn't let me leave.

I have to keep it to myself. A secret. That's the only way.

I force myself not to cry as I give Mom an extra-big hug. She lets out a confused chuckle.

"What's that for?" she asks.

"Just because," I say.

I find Neal in the hallway. His hair is still sticking up from sleep.

He grins at me. "Hey, booger brains."

I give him a jumbo-sized hug. "See ya later, slug face."

For a few strained heartbeats, I remember the shock waves that rattled our family after Dad's disappearance.

Mom did her best to hide her pain. To remain strong, cheerful, extra-organized. To act as if everything was okay. But sometimes I would catch a glimpse of her when she thought nobody was watching. And I would see the way her face crumbled with grief. The tears streaming down her cheeks. The thunderstorm of sadness. Then she would wipe away her tears, put on a big smile, and go back to being our upbeat, exceptional mom.

And Neal. He was only six when Dad left. In the weeks and months that followed, he asked so many questions. His young mind trying to understand something that couldn't be understood. *Where did Papa go? Did we do something to make him leave? Do you think he'll bring us presents when he comes back?*

I don't know what was harder: trying to find answers to his questions, or the day he stopped asking them.

I'm not just doing this for me. Or for Dad. I'm also doing it for them.

For Mom and Neal.

On my way out the door, I cast one last look at them, wondering if we'll ever see each other again.

———

Fred's waiting for me at the front curb in his unicorn backpack. "I still don't understand why you insist on going to school," he says. "Why not go directly to Legendtopia?"

"I wish I could. But if I don't show up at school, they'll call my mom. And then she might go looking for me. It's better to wait till after school. Then we just need to find a way to sneak past the Sorceress so we can go back to your world and start looking for my dad."

Fred clears his throat. "I've been meaning to speak to you about that. I understand your desire to find your father. But I really must insist that you leave this task to someone more capable."

I stop walking. "Like who?"

"Like, well . . ." Fred straightens a bit. *"Me."*

"Thanks for the offer, but this is *my* dad we're talking about. I'm not gonna just step back and let someone else go looking for him."

"I don't think you understand. This journey could be dangerous. Full of mystery and peril. And you're just a—"

I narrow my eyes. "Just a *what?*"

"Well . . . a *girl.*"

"And what's wrong with that?"

"Please don't be insulted. Girls are good at a great number of things. Dancing and sewing and arranging dinner parties—"

I let out a noise that's somewhere between a snort and a laugh. Let's call it a *snaff.* "You can't be serious!"

"But when it comes to epic quests and perilous rescue missions, you need a real man." Fred places one foot on the curb and puffs out his chest like he's posing for a royal portrait.

"Real heroic." I roll my eyes. "Did you forget you're still wearing a sparkly unicorn backpack?"

"What's wrong with unicorns? They remind me of home."

"I'm just saying, I'm gonna find my dad whether you approve or not. So you can either help me or you can—"

My voice falters. I've just caught sight of something

in the distance. Something that makes our conversation seem suddenly pointless.

The sky is blue and cloudless as far as I can see. Except for one spot. A swirl of dark clouds that stands out against the clear sky like a bruise. The clouds hover high above, churning.

After a confused moment, Fred turns and follows my gaze. His mouth drops open. He speaks in a slow, bewildered voice, as if every word is a question of its own.

"What? Is? That?"

I shake my head. The strange weather pattern looks sort of like a slow-motion tornado. One thing's for sure—this definitely *isn't* your regular, run-of-the-mill cloud. No way. There's something spooky—something sinister—about the slowly swirling funnel of dark clouds in the blue September sky.

"Perhaps it's smoke," Fred whispers. "From the fire yesterday."

He could be right. The gray splotch is hovering right around where Legendtopia is located.

But the fire happened yesterday. Shouldn't the smoke have cleared out by now?

"Let's just go," I say finally. "Don't wanna be late."

When we arrive at school, Fred and I are celebrities. And not in a good way. Everyone knows what happened at Legendtopia. I can feel their eyes following us. A couple of kids even pull out their phones and snap pictures. Walking through the front doors and down the hallway, we're trailed by a hundred different comments—

"They're the ones who started the fire!"

"And hijacked the field trip!"

"Hey, Kara—who's your boyfriend?"

"Is the new kid wearing a girl's backpack?"

I guess Prince Fred's used to attention, because he strolls down the hall like he's in the middle of a royal parade. Any second now, I'm sure he'll start waving to the crowd. I don't feel nearly as comfortable. But I keep plodding forward, trying not to trip over my own feet.

I flinch when a hand shoots out of the crowd and grabs me by the sleeve.

"Kara!"

I whirl sideways and see Marcy grinning back at me.

"There you are!" she says. "I've been trying to talk to you for, like, ever. Why didn't you answer my texts?"

"Sorry. It's just—things got a little . . ." My eyes dart in Fred's direction. "Unusual."

Marcy follows my look. When she notices Fred, her grin widens. Her braces gleam in the light.

"Hi, I'm Marcy."

She extends her arm for a handshake. Prince Fred sweeps forward and kisses her hand.

"Oh!" Marcy's face turns the color of a ripe tomato. "Uh . . . okay."

"Greetings, Marcy!" Fred declares in his most princely voice. "Enchanted to meet you. My name is Fred."

Marcy giggles. "You're not from around here, are you, Fred?"

"You are absolutely correct. I come from a faraway kingdom—"

I shoot Prince Fred a *shut-up-and-let-me-do-the-talking* look.

"Uh . . . what he means is—he's an exchange student," I say. "From England."

"Cool," says Marcy.

"Yes," Fred replies. "I suppose it *does* get cold there—"

"No, not cool like *cold*. I mean cool like, *that's awesome.*"

"I see." Prince Fred leans forward to get a closer look at Marcy's braces. "Pardon me, but might I inquire about your metal teeth?"

Marcy's hand pops up to her mouth. "My *what?*"

"He's kidding." I grab Prince Fred by the elbow. "Actually, we're running super late. We really need to get going."

Marcy stares at me like I've lost my mind. "At least tell me what really happened yesterday."

"I will. I promise. But I can't right now."

As I drag the prince backward, he waves at Marcy.

"I shall look forward to seeing you again," he calls. "Goodbye, Marcy! Farewell!"

I yank the prince sideways and pull him into the empty band hall.

"What was *that* all about?" I snap.

The prince blinks back at me innocently. "I was merely being courteous. In my world, when a young gentleman meets a young lady, he treats her with polite affection. Even *if* that lady has teeth made of metal."

I shake my head. A conversation with Prince Fred is like running an obstacle course. "I'm just saying—the whole point is to blend in. Do you think you can do that?"

But Fred doesn't answer. Because right then, our conversation is interrupted by a noise somewhere outside.

THWUMP!

Fred's jaw drops and his eyes flicker over my shoulder. I spin, following his gaze to the row of windows. A shadow ripples at the edge of one window. A gargantuan gray shape.

Then it's gone.

Prince Fred

"Did you *see* that?"

Kara's attention is trained on the window. And so is mine. Whatever's out there has vanished from view. But I can still see it in my mind. A massive gray shape lurking outside.

I flinch at the sound of Kara's voice. "What was it?"

"Hopefully nothing."

"Yeah." Kara shivers. "Hopefully."

We watch the window for a moment longer, but everything looks normal. Perhaps it really *was* nothing.

By the time we step back into the hallway, nearly everyone is gone. A few late students race to their classrooms.

But Kara doesn't act rushed. Her focus is elsewhere. She casts her gaze in one direction, then the other.

"Do you see anything out of the ordinary?" she asks.

I check my surroundings. The stone walls are lined with locked compartments. A banner hangs from the ceiling: LET'S GO, PANTHERS!

"Everything is out of the ordinary," I whisper back.

Kara sighs. "You know what I'm talking about."

"I don't see any enormous gray monsters, if that's what you mean. Not at the moment, anyway."

"That's comforting."

Our footsteps tap quietly against the floor. I tug nervously at the sparkling strap of my purple knapsack.

"Are you quite certain we should go to class?" I ask.

"At least there we won't be alone," Kara says. "And the teacher will be there, just in case. . . ."

Kara lets the thought fade into silence. But I can fill in where she left off. *Just in case something terrible happens. Just in case several hundred children face whatever peril lurks outside. Just in case the Sorceress's minions decide to enroll at Shady Pines Middle School.*

"Almost there." Kara points a finger straight down the broad, vacant hallway. "Class is that way."

We're approaching the room when I hear a rumbling.

BOOM!

BANG!

THWACK!

With every impact, the floor shakes. Kara and I stagger to a halt. I have no idea what's making all that noise, but one thing I *am* sure of: it's getting closer.

The thunderous crashing is joined by an entirely new sound. A woman's voice, which reverberates throughout the hall.

"WE ARE EXPERIENCING MINOR TREMORS. ALL STUDENTS AND STAFF SHOULD REMAIN INSIDE YOUR ROOMS."

I glance around wildly. Is this the Sorceress's spell? Is she projecting her voice across space? It doesn't *sound* like the Sorceress, but perhaps that's part of the trick.

Kara brings a hand down on my arm. "Relax. It's just the intercom."

"Inter-com? What in the seven moons is that?"

"It's a way for one person to talk to everyone in school. Through speakers. Happens all the time here. That was the principal. She must've heard the same sounds. And felt them, too."

The intercom blasts through the hallway again:

"TEACHERS, PLEASE CARRY OUT THE

URTH-QUAKE GUIDELINES. THIS IS NOT A DRILL. I REPEAT: THIS—IS—NOT—A—DRILL. IF YOU AREN'T IN YOUR CLASS ALREADY, PLEASE REPORT THERE IMMEDIATELY."

The rumbling continues, growing louder with each moment. And it sounds quite a lot like . . .

Footsteps.

Extremely massive footsteps from extremely massive feet.

"Come on." Kara sets out running. "We should get to class. Now."

I race to catch up. The hallway blurs around me. My unicorn backpack bounces against my shoulders.

My first day of school has not even begun, and already it's a disaster. The crashing sounds thud in my ears. The entire school shakes and rattles.

All of a sudden, Kara skids to a halt. She points straight ahead. At the end of the hallway, a pair of shadows takes shape against the wall. They look vaguely human—arms, legs, stomachs—but the proportions are all off. The shoulders are too broad. The hands are too thick.

Besides, no human is *that* big.

The enormous shadows edge forward against the wall. Any second now, they're going to turn the corner.

"Quick! In here!"

Kara yanks me into the nearest door. The boys' bathroom. We huddle against the wall, listening to the massive footsteps getting louder and louder. Closer and closer.

When it sounds like the monsters are just on the other side of the door, they come to a stop. I hold my breath. A frightened voice inside my head chants: *Please don't come in. Please don't come in. Please don't come in.*

They don't come in. Instead, the monsters strike up a conversation. I can hear them through the door speaking in voices that sound like boulders being ground together.

"SORCERESS SAYS THE PRINCE IZ HERE SOMEWHERE," says one.

"REMEMBER, WE'RE NOT S'POS'D TO KILL HIM," says the other. "SORCERESS SAY WE GOTTA CAPTURE HIM."

"BUT I'M HUNGRY," the first moans. "AND KIDS TASTE THE BEST."

"MAYBE WE JUST HAVE A SNACK."

"LIKE AN ARM OR SOMETHING?"

"EXACTLY!"

"GOOD IDEA!"

What is the Sorceress up to? Why does she care about capturing me?

"COME ON," says the gravelly voice. "LETZ KEEP LOOKING."

The footsteps begin pounding the floor again, moving farther away. And they probably would've kept on going if it weren't for a noise that rings out beside me.

A jingling chime.

It only lasts for a second, but that's more than enough time to send a wave of alarm across my skin. Especially when the noise comes again. And again. And *again*. Repeatedly shattering the silence of the bathroom. I glance around until I locate the source of the noise.

"Your pants!" I hiss. "They're beeping."

Kara frantically reaches into her pocket and yanks out her Self-Own. Right on cue, the horrid device erupts with another loud chime. The screen illuminates with rows of words.

"It's Marcy," Kara whispers. "She's texting me."

In a panic, I read each line of Marcy's strangely spelled and oddly punctuated texts:

Where r u???????

Ur already n trouble. This is NOT the time to skip class

BTW, that foreign xchange student is soooooo cute

Does he have a girlfriend????

125

Kara flips a button and the Self-Own goes silent. But by now it's too late. Footsteps are thundering in our direction again.

A moment later, the door flies off its hinges and a massive gray figure smashes through. I stare up at the intruder as fear sizzles through my brain.

An ogre has just crashed into the boys' bathroom.

The monstrous beast stands nearly twice the size of an ordinary man, with legs like tree trunks and massive, muscular arms. Its skin is a revolting gray color. It opens its mouth, revealing a set of teeth—each as big as my fist.

The ogre's dark, glassy eyes fix on the spot where Kara and I are crouched. Then it unleashes a mighty bellow and charges in our direction.

I stagger sideways just in time to avoid being crushed by the creature's massive foot. The next attack comes a moment later. A gargantuan gray hand swings in my direction. Kara and I dive backward and instead, the ogre punches a toilet.

The toilet explodes into a thousand porcelain shards. Water spews across the floor.

"RAAARGH!"

The ogre's roar echoes across the bathroom. A fist

collides with the tiled floor. Another smashes into a sink. More water gushes across the floor.

In the flash of a moment, I glimpse an opening. The ogre's momentum has carried it sideways, crashing into the wall. This leaves a path to the gaping hole where the bathroom door had once been.

"This way!"

Grabbing Kara's hand, I dash for the exit. As we race past the ogre, it spins to pursue us. But we're too quick for the big, clumsy creature. Its feet slip on the watery floor. Both its legs kick out in opposite directions. Thick gray arms fling to either side. And for half a second, the ogre looks like the world's biggest (and ugliest) ballerina, twirling among the toilet stalls.

Then it collapses to the floor.

Kara and I continue our race for the doorway. Our feet *splish* and *splash* with each step.

Before Kara reaches the door, however, she's greeted by the ogre's friend. This one looks just as colossal and terrifying as the first. The only difference is, it has on a very large shirt. On the front of the shirt, in big, stretched-out letters, are the words—

I HAD A LEGENDARY TIME AT LEGENDTOPIA

The ogre's huge gray hand grabs Kara.

"GOTCHA!" The creature's mouth twists into a grotesque grin. Its dark, glassy eyes gleam with malicious amusement.

"Ahhh!" Kara twists to free herself. But it's no use. Buried within the ogre's grasp, her arm looks like a twig that could snap at any second.

Paralyzed with fear, my brain catapults backward a day. Before I ever met Kara. Before I journeyed to Urth. All the way back to the tedious session with the wheezing old tutor. Learning about my brave and noble ancestors. Men who ruled Heldstone with honor and courage.

When King Frederick the Fierce was battling an army of trolls, did his emotions ever swell with as much fear as I feel right now? Was there ever a moment when King Frederick the Giant Killer wanted to curl up in a ball and cry? And what about King Frederick the Bold? My great-great-great-great-great-great-great-great-great-great-grandfather, who wrestled bears and fell madly in love with a mermaid? Surely *he* would not simply stand here and allow an ogre to kill his friend.

But unless I do something—*right now*—that's exactly what's going to happen to Kara.

Kara

Well, that's just great. I'm about to die in the boys' bathroom.

The ogre's enormous gray hand wraps around my arm. The more I struggle, the tighter it grips me. The monster's dark eyes shine with nasty glee. It's actually enjoying this. Playing with its prey before finishing it off.

If only I'd silenced my phone. If only Marcy didn't send those texts.

If only.

A foot away, Prince Fred has gone pale. His face frozen into a blank, shocked expression.

And then something seems to click. A spark lights up his eyes. His jaw clenches with determination.

In a flash, the prince plunges his hand into the water that's pooled around our feet. When he pulls it out, he's gripping a porcelain shard—a piece of the sink that broke off when Ogre #1 smashed it. The shard is as long and sharp as a butcher's knife.

Prince Fred raises the white blade above his head. And in a voice that echoes against the tile walls, he hollers:

"You shall regret the day you encountered Prince Frederick the Fourteenth, foul beast!"

Then he thrusts the shard into the ogre's foot.

"BLAAAARGHH!"

Letting out a howl of pain, the ogre releases its grip. I fall sideways, into the hall. My arm feels like it's covered with fire ants, but at least nothing seems to be broken.

Meanwhile, the prince is still stuck in the bathroom. Ogre #2 towers over him. And with a porcelain shard submerged halfway into its foot, the creature looks pretty ticked off.

"STUPID PRINCE!" it groans, hopping on its uninjured foot. "I DON'T CARE WHAT SORCERESS WANTS! I'M GONNA EAT YOU WHOLE!"

The ogre lunges. Rolling to the side, Prince Fred splashes across the watery floor. Then he springs to his feet and bolts under the monster's grasp. Past the row of shattered sinks and out the gaping hole where the door had once been.

We take off sprinting down the hall.

Somewhere behind me, I can hear the ogres smashing out of the wrecked bathroom and lumbering toward us. Their huge feet pound the floor.

SMACK! . . . SMACK! . . . SMACK!

On both sides of the hallway, classroom doors are closed. Everyone else in school is probably crouched under a desk with their hands covering their heads. All the noises, all the demolition—they must still think this is an earthquake.

I guess that makes slightly more sense than reality. Two ogres playing the world's deadliest game of tag with a couple of students.

Prince Fred and I bolt through the main doors—*correction:* the place where the main doors *used to be*. Now the entire front entryway is a tangle of twisted metal and broken glass.

The moment we burst outside, I see the cloud formation in the sky. The slow-motion tornado. It's grown over the last twenty minutes. Now the slowly swirling gray mass occupies even more of the blue sky.

But this isn't the time to worry about the weather. Fred

and I keep running. Down the sidewalk and across the bus lane, I set off in the direction of Pevensie Park. It's our best shot at survival.

If we make it that far.

I can hear the massive footsteps behind me, getting louder with each second.

The park is straight ahead. Just a little farther. Every stride brings us closer and closer and—

Prince Fred shrieks. An instant later, I realize why.

A unicorn is galloping across the grass.

I recognize it from Legendtopia. Of course, the last time I saw the unicorn, it was nothing more than a horse doll with a horn duct-taped to its forehead.

Now ... *not so much.*

The unicorn is bigger and badder in every way. Its white fur shines in the sunlight. Muscles flex and strain as it runs. Even with nacho cheese splattered across its haunches, the creature looks impressive. Its white horn is much longer and sharper—and *definitely* isn't being held on by duct tape.

I don't know about you, but when I think of a unicorn, I imagine a creature frolicking in a meadow. Maybe a rainbow in the background. A pleasant stream trickling nearby.

But this unicorn doesn't match that description *at all.*

Its thick hooves pound the earth, tearing up huge chunks of grass. Nostrils flaring, teeth gnashing. Horn jutting out like a spear. It looks like it just escaped from the world's most dangerous magical rodeo and is ready to kill anything in its path.

And it's headed straight for us.

There's nowhere to hide. No escape. If we keep running in the same direction, we'll probably get skewered by a unicorn's horn. But turning around will only send us straight into the arms of the ogres.

We're trapped. We're doomed. We're . . .

My eyes land on Fred's backpack. The little cartoon unicorns seem especially ridiculous now that we're about to get killed by an *actual* unicorn. But the sight also gives me an idea.

"Our backpacks!" I scream.

"What about them?" Fred screams back.

"We can use them! As weapons!"

A hopeful look blazes in Fred's eyes. He yanks away his backpack and I do the same.

The unicorn is closing in on us. The point of its horn gleams in the sunlight as it speeds toward my chest.

Without slowing down, I swing my backpack. It strikes the unicorn in the eye.

The creature releases a surprised "*Neeeeiiighhhh!*" Prince

Fred swings and hits it with his own backpack. The blow thrusts its head sideways. At the speed the unicorn's moving, the double impact is enough to knock it off balance.

The creature collapses to the ground. Grass and unicorn slobber fly everywhere.

I can't believe it! Our attack worked! But it's too early to start celebrating. We're still being followed by two ogres. And they're gaining ground fast. The monster with the injured foot is lagging behind. Unfortunately, the other is closer.

Much closer.

The ogre reaches out with one massive gray hand. I attempt another swing with my backpack. But this time, the strategy doesn't work so well. The ogre snatches the backpack out of the air and crushes it within its thick fingers.

"NEXT THING I SMASH GONNA BE YER HEAD!" the ogre grunts.

Just a little farther. On the other side of the road is the park. My feet pound the street. My heart booms in my ears.

The ogre growls as it makes another grab. A streak of gray. Its huge grip closes in on me.

Prince Fred

Another second, and we would've made a nice meal for a couple of ogres. Instead, we crash into the woods.

Suddenly, branches are everywhere. Leaves slap me in the face. My legs slip out from under me and I slide down a muddy ravine. Kara's beside me. Tripping, falling, sliding. When we hit the bottom, I tumble onto my side. Kara helps me up, and we keep running.

Sounds explode all around us. Footsteps pummeling the dirt, branches snapping, rasping breaths. We dodge trees, veer around knotted vines, leap over stumps.

When we finally come to a stop, we take cover between a few thick bushes. I bend over, hands on my knees, gulping for air.

Every inch of my body hurts. My lungs burn, my arms are covered in scratches, my legs ache from all the running. Growing up in the Royal Palace, I was always kept safe and protected. Whenever I tripped, someone was there to catch me. Whenever I climbed on tables, someone was there to gently lower me to the floor.

Pain is a new sensation for me. And I don't like it very much.

THWACK! CLOMP! CRAAACK!

The ogres' footsteps pound the forest floor. I duck lower, hoping the trees and bushes will keep us hidden. Through the branches, I can just barely see their huge gray legs come into view. A porcelain shard pokes out of one foot. The beast with the injured foot turns in our direction. It sniffs loudly.

"YOU SMELL SOMETHIN'?"

"NOW THATCHA MENTION IT . . . I DO."

I hold my breath. Inside my brain, there's a shouting match taking place. One side is screaming, *Run! Run! Run!* The other's yelling at an equal volume. *Stay! Stay! Stay!* Both options seemed equally logical. And equally dangerous.

"YEAH, I SMELL SOMETHIN', ALL RIGHT." The first ogre sniffs. "SMELLS LIKE . . . YER BUTT!"

And then it bursts into a round of atrocious grunts of laughter. The injured ogre seems less amused.

"THIS NO TIME FOR JOKES!" it growls. "WE GOTTA FIND THAT PRINCE!"

The other chokes down the last of its laughter. "WHY'S THE SORCERESS WANT THE PRINCE SO BAD, ANYWAY?"

"'CAUSE HE'S HANDSOME."

Handsome? Did the ogre just call me handsome?

I appreciate the compliment, but what does that have to do with anything?

"SHE NOT SAY HANDSOME," corrects the other ogre. "SHE SAY HE'S SOMETHING ELSE. SOMETHING THAT *SOUND* LIKE HANDSOME."

"GANSOME? PANTSUM?"

"NO. THAT NOT IT, EITHER."

"ZANSOM?"

"OOH! I REMEMBER!" The ogre jumps up and down with excitement. Tremors shake the ground. "SORCERESS SAY THE PRINCE IS *RANSOM!*"

The ogre with the injured foot grunts its agreement. "OF COURSE! RANSOM! THAT MAKE PERFECT SENSE!"

A brief silence fills the conversation. And then—

"UH . . . WHAT *RANSOM* MEAN?"

"NO IDEA."

"ME NEITHER."

I, however, am quite familiar with the term. The Sorceress wishes to hold me hostage, to use me as bait, to lure my father into giving her anything and everything she wants.

The question is . . . *What does the Sorceress want?*

Soon, the ogres continue on their way. As they clomp through the forest, their plodding footsteps fade. I'm about to step out of our hiding spot when a different noise grabs my attention. A rustle in the bushes. I spin, skin tingling with nerves. All my fear fizzles away when I see what made the noise.

A fat little frog.

I take a calming breath. Unicorns and ogres are one thing. But frogs? We can handle frogs.

My relief lasts a total of three seconds. Right up until the moment that the little amphibian opens its mouth and begins to speak.

Kara

I must be hearing things. The stress of the past few hours is finally getting to me. There's no other way to explain what happens next. An ordinary-looking frog hops onto the path, opens its mouth, and croaks a word.

A word that sounds exactly like "Hello."

It can't be. I must be losing my mind.

Except if that's the case, why does Fred look so freaked out?

"D-did you hear that?" I ask.

The prince nods.

We both turn back to the frog. It looks up at us with its little froggy eyes. A long moment passes. And just when I'm starting to convince myself that it really *was* just my imagination, the fat little frog opens its mouth and croaks—

"My name is Frog."

"Uh . . . Kara," Prince Fred mutters. "I thought you said the creatures of your world can't talk."

"They can't," I say.

"This frog seems to disagree with you."

"My name is Frog," the frog says again.

"The Sorceress," Prince Fred mutters. "She must be behind this."

"But how? Pevensie Park is nowhere near Legendtopia. She'd need some way of enchanting them beyond the walls of—"

And then I realize. The cloud. The slow-motion tornado. It's been growing all morning. Increasing in size. When I gaze up through the branches, I can see it. Looming in the sky. Dark and churning. And definitely coming from Legendtopia.

I point at the swirling black mass in the sky. "That's how she's doing it. That isn't a cloud, and it isn't smoke. It's"—I search for the right description—"it's, like, magical pollution."

Fred tilts a disbelieving glance my way. "Magical *what?*"

"It's like the Sorceress's evil magic is pouring out of Legendtopia. Into the air, into the water. It's spreading."

"And that includes frogs?"

"Exactly."

Croak. "My name is Frog."

When I look at the frog again, it isn't alone. Now there are several. A dozen, at least. More and more of them hopping out of the bushes with each passing second, their voices croaking out the most mundane conversation I've ever heard.

"My name is Frog."

"My name is also Frog."

"My name is Frog, too."

"I am also named Frog."

Sheesh. These frogs may have figured out how to talk, but they don't have anything interesting to say.

"I am Frog."

"That is what I am also called."

"Me too."

There must be fifty of them by this point. Maybe more. They come in all different shapes and sizes. Big and small, fat and slim, warty and extra-warty. Their moist little eyes blink up at us, their necks bulging. It's getting creepy.

I edge closer to the prince. Frogs crowd us on all sides. My eyes land on the biggest of the group. It's about the size of a softball, with bumpy brownish-green skin.

With a croak of effort, the creature rises onto its hind legs. For a moment, the frog wobbles like a newborn who's just learned to stand. Its belly bulges out in front.

As the biggest—and the only one standing upright— the massive amphibian looks to be the leader of the group. The other frogs turn to watch it. And then, one by one, they mimic their leader's actions. They rise to their feet.

Big Guy flaps his webbed hands and the chorus of croaks comes to a stop. The park goes eerily quiet. Opening his mouth, Big Guy speaks in a deep, revolting voice. And this time, he has something very different to say.

"We are frogs and this is our forest." His wet eyes slowly move from me to Fred. "You are invaders and you must be punished."

The frog beside him is the next to speak up.

"Invaders must be punished!" it says. "Invaders must be punished!"

A few more frogs join in. Their croaking voices combine into a chant.

"Invaders must be punished! Invaders must be punished!"

Soon, the entire crowd of frogs is reciting the same lines—

"Invaders must be punished! Invaders must be punished!"

Even though a big part of me finds this whole situation totally freaky, there's also something funny about it. Are we really getting threatened by . . . *a bunch of frogs?*

I can't help chuckling. But Prince Fred doesn't see the humor in it.

"This isn't something to jest about," he warns. "These creatures may be small, but they vastly outnumber us."

"You can't be serious." I cast a lopsided grin at the chanting amphibian mob. "If we could handle ogres and a killer unicorn, I think we can deal with a few slimy little fr—ouch!"

One of the frogs just grabbed a pointed rock and launched it with surprising force. The rock smacked me right beneath the eye.

Maybe it's not so funny after all. Especially now that another rock just sailed through the air and collided with my forehead.

More of the frogs are getting in on the act now. Grabbing

whatever they can find—twigs, pebbles, clumps of dirt—and throwing them at us. The mob surrounds us on all sides, inching closer and closer.

I shriek when a sharp stick hits my arm like a mini-spear. "We have to get out of here!"

But when I try to step over the frogs, they grab hold of my pant legs. A few begin scaling the inside of my pants.

"Aaaugh!" I scream, swatting them away. "Yuck! Gross!"

"Curse these tiny devils!" A bunch more frogs are treating Fred's leg like it's their own personal climbing wall. "I command you to cease this assault!"

"We do not take orders from humans!" croaks the leader frog. "This is our forest! All invaders must be punished!"

I kick my leg and send a few frogs flying. "We're not *invading* anything!"

But the frogs aren't listening. They crowd the path, violently hurling rocks and sticks at us. Their croaks sound like battle cries. Their slimy hands reach for us from every direction.

I spot a tree branch hanging over the path above me. Jumping, I'm able to grasp the branch and snap it off. I swing the branch, its bushy leaves sweeping the frogs aside like a broom. This clears a path through the frog army.

Fred follows close behind. Smacking a few more frogs out of the way, I hurry down the path. The frogs hop after us with surprising speed.

"Over here!" I point to my left, where the path forks and leads to an opening with a playground.

We stumble over a stretch of grass and onto the playground. The sound of chanting frog voices fades behind us. When I turn around, I realize why. The frogs stopped chasing us. They're lined up at the edge of the path, watching. One of them accidentally stumbles onto the playground, but instantly scrambles back to the path.

"This day just keeps getting weirder." I hunch forward, catching my breath. "At least those little jerks aren't following us anymore."

"But why?" Fred casts a suspicious look back the way we came. Fifty frogs are lined up at the edge of the playground. "Why would they just suddenly . . . *stop?*"

"Who cares? As long as they're not in my pants, I'm not complaining."

The prince's forehead wrinkles. "Do the frogs look nervous to you? Afraid?"

"They look *slimy*." I shudder at the memory of their nasty little webbed hands. "Now, will you stop psychoanalyzing frogs. We've got bigger things to worry about. Like the evil magic pollution cloud that's turning this entire town crazy."

"Perhaps you're right." Fred shifts his attention away from the frogs. "But what can we do?"

I shrug. We're just kids. We can't possibly take on the Sorceress and her evil army. We're better off marching straight to the police station and letting them take over from here.

But what are we supposed to say? *Excuse me, but an evil witch from another world is taking over. She's transforming Legendtopia into her own personal fortress and turning frogs into violent little jerks.*

Yeah, I'm sure that'll go over *real* well.

Besides, the Sorceress would just brainwash anyone who tries to confront her. Just like she did with the fire-fighters.

I stare at the padded playground floor, frustration piling up inside me. A mountain of reasons why our mission is hopeless. And yet . . .

And yet we can't just sit back and let some evil witch take over our town, our country, our world. We have to fight back—now—while we still stand a tiny little chance.

For about half a second, I'm feeling all gung-ho and ready for battle.

That all vanishes with a wrenching metallic groan. I spin around, and instantly realize—Fred was right earlier. There *was* a reason why the frogs stopped chasing us. They must've known the danger we were stumbling into. And now that danger is becoming real.

The playground is coming to life.

Prince Fred

Until today, I didn't know what a "play-ground" was. And now one is trying to kill us.

The support beams rip loose from the padded ground, tearing out chunks of gravel. The play-ground transforms into an enormous lumbering monster.

It stomps toward us on a dozen stiff metal legs. Red and yellow bars gnash together like teeth. The slide flops up and down like a slobbering tongue. A tail of climbing chains rattles behind it. The play-ground is a heartbeat away from landing on top of me with all its weight when Kara screams—

"Get outta there!"

She rams me with her shoulder. The two of us tumble

to the padded ground just as a bright red support beam pummels the exact spot where I'd just been standing.

There's no time to thank Kara. She's scrambling to her feet. And so am I. We begin running, but instantly stagger to a halt when the play-ground slumps into our path.

The groan of twisting metal and plastic echoes across the clearing. Before I can make another move, the slide stretches forward—an enormous, disgusting red tongue that wraps around my ankle.

"Aggghh!" I kick and squirm, but it's no use. The slide only tightens around my leg. I look up at Kara. "Get out of here while you still have a chance!"

"I'm not leaving you!" Kara yells. "Just stay calm!"

How in the seven moons am I supposed to "stay calm" when a monster play-ground is about to devour me? The thing slouches forward, its multicolored bars clamping together like the jaws of a hungry predator.

"Grab hold!"

Kara takes my hand and pulls. With my free foot, I kick the slide again and again and again.

"Let!" SMACK! "Go!" WHAP! "Of!" CLONK! "Me!"

The final kick loosens the slide's hold enough for me to wrench my leg loose. Kara helps me to my feet and we stumble away.

"Watch out for the monkey bars!" Kara screams.

"What are monkey ba—*oof!*"

A row of horizontal metal bars slams me in the shoulder. I have a feeling *they* are monkey bars. On my feet again, I stagger forward until we've managed to put some distance between ourselves and the monster play-ground. With the sounds of wrenching plastic and metal trailing us, Kara and I race toward the edge of the clearing. We're nearly there when a yellow-and-gray blur appears at the edge of my vision.

Beside me, Kara yelps. "Oh, crud! It's the swing set!"

On ordinary occasions, I imagine the "swing set" might be quite a lot of fun. But at this moment, it looks deadly. It lumbers toward us, a riot of clinking and squeaking and clanking. Chains twist and slither like snakes.

"Come on!" I yell. "We must keep moving!"

"No need to tell me twice!"

We bolt to the edge of the clearing. Past the tree line and onto the path, we don't slow down until the sounds of the monster play-ground have faded.

Kara leans against a vine-covered tree to catch her breath. "I'm never coming back to this park again."

"But it's not just the park," I remind her. "Soon your entire village will be infected with the Sorceress's evil enchantment. We must journey to Legendtopia. To the source of the Sorceress's power."

"Oh, right. What should we do after that? Knock on the door and ask the evil witch lady if she'll stop trying to take over the world?"

"I know this is a perilous quest," I say through gritted teeth. "But it's our only choice. We have to stop the Sorceress. Before she gets any stronger."

"This isn't just about the Sorceress." Kara fixes me in an unwavering gaze. "It's also about my dad."

"Please don't tell me you're still planning on going after him."

"Of course I am." As she speaks, Kara pulls her necklace out of her pocket. The chain dangles from her fist. Her thumb absently rubs the silver owl. "My dad's out there. Being held prisoner in your world. I have to find him. I have to bring him back."

The strange thing is . . . a part of me actually admires Kara's bravery. Even if it *is* likely to get her killed.

"Very well. Then we'll go together." I puff out my chest grandly. "A quest to save the kingdom of Urth and rescue your father! It shall be epic!"

Kara rolls her eyes. "I totally get why Marcy has a crush on you."

I glance away, feeling my cheeks turn red. "This is . . . er—no time for romance. Besides, I'm not interested in girls with metal teeth. Now let's keep moving. This forest is full of dangers."

"It's not a forest. It's just a little park."

Perhaps Kara's comment was true once. But all that's changed now. The Sorceress has transformed the park into something else entirely. Something dark and evil.

Kara

The park is like an enchanted obstacle course. We approach a stream that I've walked past a million times before—except now, the rushing water is blood-red and boiling. Avoiding the lava rapids, Fred stumbles toward a raggedy-looking bush. He falls backward when the bush reaches for him, a humongous claw going for the world's deadliest high five.

"Watch out!" I yank Fred away from the grasping branches. "This whole park's trying to kill us!"

"Is that so?" Fred shields his face as the trees began pelting us with acorns. "I'd failed to notice until your astute observation!"

At least the prince is finally starting to figure out sarcasm.

Pevensie Park has become a maze. The path zigzags in strange directions. Tangles of vines block out the sunlight, making it impossible to see more than a few feet in front of me.

Then I catch sight of it. A glimmer. Barely more than a glowing dot. But in the darkness, it's like a spotlight.

"This way!"

I switch directions, plunging toward the light. Fred staggers to keep up. As we get closer, the glow intensifies. Acorns rain down from above. Birds swoop from low branches. I'm worried they're planning to fly in our faces, but they have something else in mind. Something much worse.

"Watch out!" I scream. "It's a poop attack!"

Fred ducks, covering his head. "Ugh! How revolting!"

We manage to escape the birds (and their poop), but we're not out of the woods yet. Up ahead, a few dozen frogs have emerged from the bushes. And they're back to their stupid chant.

"Invaders must be punished!"

"Invaders must be punished!"

In their slimy hands, the frogs are holding little spears.

They line up in front of us, blocking the path. Their croaking voices overwhelm all other noise.

"Invaders must be punished!"

The frogs raise their spears . . .

Take aim . . .

And launch their weapons . . .

Thirty mini-spears fly in our direction. I guard my face with my hands. It feels like running straight into a storm of toothpicks. But at least I manage to block any of the spears from getting in my eyes or down my throat.

With a huge jump, I clear the battalion of frogs and crash through the thicket. Branches slash at my face and arms. But my momentum carries me through, and I land in the open.

No more dirt path. Now I'm racing across sidewalk. I can hear Fred's footsteps and his rapid breathing beside me.

After being surrounded by darkness, the sudden flood of sunlight is blinding. But I don't let that stop me. I keep running, blood pumping with adrenaline, until I'm more than a block from the park.

When we get to a traffic light, we stumble to a stop. I reach into my pocket and grab my phone.

"What are you doing?" Fred asks.

"Calling my mom," I say. With the supposed earthquake, and the fact that I never actually made it to first period, there's a good chance the school has called my mom. I need to talk to her. Tell her I'm okay—at least for the time being.

But it's impossible to make the call. My phone's acting totally glitchy. The screen flickers. The icons seem to be shrinking. Growing dimmer and dimmer, like pennies disappearing into a pool of water. Until they're gone. Swallowed by the dark screen.

I swipe my thumb across the screen again, but nothing happens.

"That's weird," I say. "My phone's not working."

Fred peers at the screen. "How odd. Do you think it has anything to do with—?"

"The Sorceress?" I shove the useless phone back into my pocket. "That'd be my first guess."

It's one thing to send fantasy creatures rampaging through town, but mess with people's phones? That's taking it too far. The Sorceress needs to be stopped.

At least we won't need GPS to find our way to Legendtopia. The swirling dark cloud in the sky is like the world's biggest billboard: EVIL MAGIC THIS WAY!!! The black funnel is enormous, looming over everything. A giant, creepy V that emerges straight from Legendtopia.

Turning away from the toxic-magic pollution cloud, my eyes land on a more welcome sight. A gas station. I lead the prince inside, where he tours the place like it's a museum. The candy bars and motor oil and magazines. It's all brand-new to him.

While Fred studies the merchandise, I stock up. Before leaving home this morning, I rummaged through my sock drawer, scrounging together the last of my birthday money. Twenty bucks. That should at least buy us some supplies. I grab bottles of water, bags of nuts, energy bars.

As we approach the counter, I come down with a sudden case of nerves. It's the middle of the morning on a school day. Our clothes are muddy and torn. Our arms and legs are covered in scratches. Basically, the two of us look like we skipped school to mud-wrestle with a panther.

But the gas station employee doesn't seem to notice. All his attention is on the TV behind the counter. The screen shows flashes of images. Video footage that looks both very familiar and very strange. A grocery store that's been completely overtaken by talking squirrels. Crows perched on a power line, cawing rude insults to anyone who walks by. Thorny vines cracking through concrete, climbing up the walls of houses, trapping residents inside.

A reporter's voice speaks over these videos: "Local authorities are baffled by the bizarre events that have gripped Shady Pines today. No word yet on the cause, though some experts are speculating that—"

The screen begins to flicker. It's just like what happened with my phone a few minutes ago. The video drops away, replaced by darkness.

"What the . . ." The employee reaches out and whacks the side of the TV. "Stupid thing's broken."

He hits it again. And again. And—

All of a sudden, a new image appears on the screen. A close-up view of a face that I've seen before.

My spine turns to ice.

The Sorceress is staring out of the TV.

Prince Fred

"Greetings, citizens of Urth."

The Sorceress speaks in a melodious voice. Her high cheekbones glimmer with a pale light. Her mouth curls into a beguiling smile. And there's something about her dark eyes. Something that makes me want to lean in closer, to take a better look.

"I have spent the past three years seeking a way into your world," she says. "And now that I am here, I wish to introduce myself. I am your sole authority. Your ruler. Your queen."

The Sorceress's eyes are like dark pools, inviting me to dive deeper and deeper. When I attempt to look away,

I . . . *can't*. No matter how hard I try, the magical current is too powerful.

In a musical voice, she repeats herself. "Your sole authority. Your ruler. Your queen."

I can feel the same words forming on my lips. Then I remember the evil in the Sorceress's heart. The terrible things she has in store for Urth. I can't allow myself to be sucked into her hypnotic spell. I clench my fists. Grind my teeth. Summon every last shred of my strength.

Must.

Turn.

Away.

At last, I manage to pull my attention from the television. Instead, I fix my gaze on the gasoline station employee. He's staring at the screen as though it's the most interesting, most captivating, most wonderful thing he's ever seen.

"My sole authority," he mutters. "My ruler. My queen."

Beside me, Kara is just as entranced with the screen. With the same faraway longing in her expression, she begins to speak in a low, lifeless whisper.

"My sole authority," she mumbles. "My ruler. My—"

"Stop watching!"

Lunging forward, I tackle Kara. The two of us collapse

to the ground. When she looks up at me, her eyes are wide and stunned.

"Hey!" she squeals. "I was watching that!"

Kara scrambles to gain a view of the television again, but I block her.

"Do you not see what's happening?" I grip her by the shoulders. "The Sorceress. She's trying to enchant you. She's trying to enchant *everyone*."

"Just a little more!" Kara tries to push me out of the way, but I won't budge. "Please!"

My grip on her shoulders tightens as I force her to look me in the eyes. "Focus on me. Just me. Nothing else."

Slowly, the life returns to her expression. Her true self, her essential Kara-ness. It is coming back. At last.

"Wh-what just happened?" she asks.

"The Sorceress. She's devised a way to mix the magic of her world with the technology of yours. She's using the television—"

"To brainwash the entire population," Kara whispers. "All at once."

The strategy is brilliant. And sinister. Precisely what you would expect from the Sorceress.

Behind the counter, the employee continues to stare

deeply into the television. Again and again, he mumbles the same thing.

"My sole authority. My ruler. My queen."

Careful to avoid glancing anywhere near the television, we load our food and water into my knapsack. Kara places her money on the counter. The employee remains utterly unaware of our presence.

Kara slides the money forward. "Uh ... keep the change, I guess."

On our way out of the gasoline station, Kara and I stagger to a halt. Outside are rows of pumps. Motorists filling their tanks with fuel. I've seen this peculiar procedure before. But never like this.

The nozzles have come to life. They squirm free of peoples' hands. They wriggle like snakes, spewing gasoline at anyone who comes near.

A motorist screams. Another backs against his car, watching the nozzle weave through the air.

But then a strange calm falls over the people. Because in that instant, they notice the small screens built into the gasoline pumps. And flickering on each screen is the same video we saw inside.

The Sorceress.

All of a sudden, the motorists are not nearly as

concerned about the chaos that has overtaken the gasoline station. They appear serene, lifeless, dull. Again and again, they chant the same words.

"My sole authority. My ruler. My queen."

All of Shady Pines is falling under the Sorceress's spell.

Kara

The Sorceress's enchantment buzzes in my memory. Her dark eyes pulling me deeper. Her steady voice luring me closer. The experience hangs over my brain like a dream. While it was happening, the connection had felt so real. But now I barely remember it at all.

If we want to have any chance of putting an end to the insanity, we'll need to stop the Sorceress. And that means we can't let anything stand in our way. We need to reach the Sorceress's new home. Her headquarters. Her castle.

Legendtopia.

Fleeing the gas station, I glance at the massive swirl of black clouds in the distance. Ordinarily, I'd be running away from weather like that. Instead, the prince and I head straight for it. The fastest route is through the Shady Pines Mall. We bolt across the street and begin making our way across the mall's parking lot when I hear a buzzing noise.

It sounds like mosquitoes.

Really *big* mosquitoes.

"Get down!" I duck between a couple of cars.

Fred crouches beside me. "What is it?"

"Shh."

I listen. And a moment later, I hear it again. *Bzzzzzz.* I peek out from behind the car's hood and that's when I see them.

At first they look like hummingbirds. A dozen little creatures flying across the parking lot on rapidly flapping wings. Except they have human bodies. Arms and legs and heads. Not to mention angry eyes and sharp little teeth.

A flock of fairies is headed our way.

Just the sight of them makes my skin crawl. The last time I saw them was back in Legendtopia. Pulling at my hair with their little hands, kicking me in the face with their little feet.

They're still unaware of our presence. At least for now. But I can hear them getting nearer. The sound of their buzzing wings grows louder and louder. Prince Fred and I keep close to the ground, shuffling as quietly as possible between cars to avoid detection.

We freeze at the sound of voices. Extremely high-pitched voices.

"*The chillldren must be arounnnd here sommmewhere,*" squeaks one of the fairies. Every syllable stretches like taffy.

"*Yesssss, but wherrre?*" replies another.

"*The froooogs say they essscaped the forrrest on fooooot. They cannnn't have gonnne farrr.*"

"*Mayyyybe they wennnt to the mall. Humannnns loooove malls.*"

"*Iffff that's true, thennnn it's already toooo late for themmm. The mall is parrrt of the Sorceress's domaaaain now. Annnd she has mmmade some wwwwonderful renovations.*"

This comment causes the entire group of fairies to burst into high-pitched laughter. Even though I can't see them, I can just imagine them rubbing their little hands together in devilish glee.

"*Come allllong,*" says the leader of the fairies. "*Let's connnntinue scouting. They'lll nnnnever make it ouuuut of the paaaarking lot.*"

The fairies fly away. Once the sound of their buzzing wings fades into silence, I turn to Prince Fred.

"It's too dangerous to stay here," I whisper. "We should find someplace to take cover."

"Yes, but . . ." Fred casts an uneasy glance at our surroundings. "Where are we supposed to go?"

Uncertainty swells inside me. My nervous habit kicks in. I grab the necklace out of my pocket, gripping it tightly in my fist. For a moment, I'm sure I feel the owl's little metal wings fluttering against my skin. But when I open my hand, it's just lying there on my palm. Motionless. An ordinary charm.

Big, blank eyes. Pointy silver beak.

I shove the owl necklace back into my pocket. "Our best option is to cut through the mall."

"Did you not hear the fairies? They say this mall has been taken over by the Sorceress."

"In case you didn't notice, the entire *town's* been taken over by the Sorceress. Besides, that's the shortest way."

Fred sighs. "Very well. Let's go to the mall."

Prince Fred

As we approach the entrance, the glass doors suddenly slide apart with a quiet *whoosh*. I grab Kara by the elbow and pull her to the side. A moment later, the doors close again.

"Perhaps we should find another entrance. This doorway has obviously been enchanted by the Sorceress." I wave my hand in front of the door and it slides open again. "See? It opens on its own!"

Despite the tense situation, Kara laughs. "That's not magic. It's an automatic door."

"Are you sure?"

"Of course. Now come on. Before one of those fairies spots us."

We slip through the entrance. Once inside, I turn around and test out the "automatic door" again. Each time I step forward, the glass doors swish open. Stepping back, they close once again. Forward—*open*. Backward—*close*. Forw—

"Quit messing around!" Kara pulls me away from the door and inside the mall.

I inspect my new surroundings with astonishment. The signs are so colorful! The shops so big and bright!

And then I notice clear proof of magical enchantment.

"Look there!" I whisper. "That staircase—it appears to be . . . moving!"

I point straight ahead. A stairway in which the steps glide up and up and up.

For the second time in the past minute, Kara laughs at me. "That's just an escalator."

I scratch my head. Doorways that open automatically? Moving staircases? Kara might insist that these things are not magical, but I disagree.

"It's weird." Kara glances around. "There are usually more people here."

She makes an excellent point. The markets of my world are always swarming with people. But here, everything is utterly and completely . . .

Vacant.

Ahead of us, the broad corridor is unpopulated. There are no people in the shops. No employees. Nobody.

"Where is everyone?" I ask.

Kara shrugs. "Maybe nobody's in the mood for shopping. Too much freaky stuff going on around town."

"Perhaps."

But even as the word leaves my lips, I have a grim feeling there's something more to it than that.

"We've already made it this far," Kara says. "Might as well keep going."

She leads the way. Past vacant shops and unoccupied benches. We've only gone a few steps when we hear the noise.

Clank-clank-CLANK!... Clank-clank-CLANK!

It sounds like silverware rattling in the distance. Except there's nothing random about the noise. More like a carefully timed pattern. And with each second, it grows louder.

Clank-clank-CLANK!... Clank-clank-CLANK!

Kara casts a nervous glance my way. "What do you think it is?"

"I haven't the slightest idea." I pause, listening, as the metallic clanking approaches. "But I would prefer not to be here when it arrives."

"Same here."

We hurry into a nearby clothing shop, where we hide behind a rack of dresses. My heart races. The rhythmic sounds get closer and closer, until each echo pounds in my skull like thunder.

Three soldiers are marching toward us. They're covered from head to toe in silver armor. The visors of their helmets have been pulled down, obscuring any view of the soldiers' faces. At their sides, each carries a sword inside a sheath.

There's no question who ordered them to patrol the mall. The Sorceress.

I have often watched the knights of Heldstone from the windows of my palace, but never have I seen anyone move with such accuracy and precision. The soldiers' steps are perfectly synchronized so that their armored boots come down at the exact same moment.

Left-right-LEFT! . . . Left-right-LEFT!

The marching continues. And when I peer out from behind the rack again, the soldiers are gone. The clockwork-clacking of their march steadily dwindles.

Beside me, Kara wipes the sweat from her forehead. "That was close."

"We should keep moving," I whisper.

But Kara has turned her attention to the rack of elegant ball gowns. She runs a finger over the purple velvet trim, knitting her brow.

"Doesn't make any sense," she mutters.

"What do you mean?"

Once again, Kara ignores me. Instead, she wanders through the store, inspecting the merchandise. Men's tunics and feathered caps, silken headdresses and linen bonnets. She pauses next to a sign that reads:

RIDING CLOAKS
50% OFF!!!

"What in the seven moons are you doing?" I ask in a harsh whisper. "This is no time to browse the fashion choices!"

Kara turns to me, bewilderment swimming in her eyes. "Don't you see?"

"See *what?*"

"Everything in this store has changed."

"I don't understand. It's a clothing store. They sell *clothing.* What's so strange about that?"

"Yeah, but . . ." Kara whirls to gaze at the racks. "This place has always sold, like, T-shirts and jeans. Now it's all stuff that went out of style a few centuries ago. Stuff from your world."

"Are you sure?"

"Of course I'm sure!" Kara points to a rack of corsets. "News flash, Fred—people don't wear corsets anymore!"

Perhaps she's right. At one corner of the store is the men's section. In another is the women's. A third part of the store is reserved for elves.

My memory hurls back to the conversation among the fairies we overheard in the parking lot. *The mall is parrrt of the Sorceress's domaaaain now,* one said. *Annnd she has mmmade some wwwwonderful renovations.*

Clearly, they weren't joking around.

Kara

⌒

Fred and I leave the store, keeping close to the wall. I listen carefully for the armored soldiers. Their steady clanking march sounds far in the distance.

Before too long, we reach one of my favorite spots in the mall—Smoothie Sensations. I almost suggest we make a quick stop for a strawberry-banana swirl. Then I notice the store's been replaced with a rickety wooden shack. Cauldrons burble behind the counter. The sign above now reads PUTRID PORRIDGE.

Looks like smoothies aren't on the menu anymore.

We keep moving. Up ahead is an electronics store, where every television, every computer monitor, every laptop and cell phone screen is displaying the same thing.

The Sorceress's face. The hypnotic message is being broadcast everywhere. Her dark eyes peer out from a hundred different screens. Her spellbinding voice blares from a hundred different speakers.

The evil witch has gone viral.

I can feel my feet trying to carry me closer. All I want is a quick look. Just enough to find out what she's saying. I'm drifting toward the electronics store, mindless, like a leaf caught in a lazy current when—

Fred grabs my hand. He pulls me away.

"You must resist!" His grip is firm. So is his voice. "Don't let her pull you in."

I take a breath. Instead of looking toward the electronics store, my eyes connect with Fred. "Thanks."

He squeezes my hand. "Better now?"

I nod. "Better."

We hurry away. Past a cell phone kiosk that now sells parchment and quills. A bookstore where the shelves are stocked with scrolls. It isn't until the electronics store is far behind us that I notice.

We're still holding hands.

Fred seems to realize this at the same moment that I do.

We both let go. My palm feels sweaty. All of a sudden, I don't know where to look. For a moment, all the craziness around us fades away. The enchanted stores. The armored soldiers lurking around. The fairies outside.

For a moment, we're just two awkward kids hanging out in the mall.

The illusion falls away when I notice the nearby pet store. The fish tanks are filled with vicious-looking water sprites. Cages that once held puppies and kittens are now home to all kinds of weird creatures, bizarre hybrids straight from the Sorceress's dark imagination. The labels attached to their cages show their names.

Chimpanzeebra. Squirrelephant. Giraffeopotamus.

I shiver. "If the Sorceress keeps working her magic, the whole world's gonna eventually look like this."

"Then we must stop her," Fred mutters through gritted teeth. "Today. Before her evil can spread any more than it already has."

We keep walking. And just when I'm beginning to think we might actually make it out of the mall without any other dangerous encounters, I hear the sound again.

Clank-clank-CLANK! . . . Clank-clank-CLANK!

The soldiers are getting closer.

We need a place to hide. I start for the Perfume Emporium. But as we approach, I notice the sign above the door. It's changed slightly.

It's not the Perfume Emporium.

It's the *Potion* Emporium.

I nearly turn back, but we don't have any other options. The soldiers will be here any second. And so Fred and I bolt into the shop.

We duck behind a shelf. As I listen to the armored soldiers clanging around outside, my eyes land on the row of glass bottles in front of me. They look like your typical perfumes. Except that the Sorceress has done a little rebranding. And now the labels advertise a whole bunch of different potions—

Horrendous Hog's Snout Serum.

Terrible Toothache Tonic.

Burning Booger Belch.

Then I catch sight of a slender glass bottle. The liquid inside glows pink. The name of the potion is written in a flowery cursive script:

Essence of Infatuary.

Inside the bottle, pink liquid bubbles and fizzes. Light shimmers against the elegant glass. It's perched on the very edge of the shelf. And with every thunderous *CLANK!* of the soldiers' footsteps, the bottle rattles closer and closer to the edge.

That thing's about to fall, I think.

I reach for it, but I'm a split second too late. The bottle tips over the edge and drops to the floor.

I manage to dive clear of the crash. Fred's not so lucky. The glass breaks and the magical potion spills out around him. As I look at him, standing in a puddle of sparkling pink liquid, all I can think to say is—

"Uh-oh."

Prince Fred

It all happens so suddenly.

In front of me is a pretty glass bottle. *Essence of Infatuary.* In my world, the Infatuary is a species of fairy. A winged creature, no taller than your thumb. Glowing pink skin. Silky yellow hair. Legend claims that the Infatuary casts a spell that makes you fall madly in love with the first person you see.

I can only assume that the Essence of Infatuary has a similar effect.

Love in a bottle.

The next thing I know, the bottle tips over and crashes to the ground. My first thought is, *I hope the soldiers didn't hear!* My second, third, and fourth thoughts are—

Move, you fool! You're standing in a pool of magic potion!!!

But it's too late. A pink mist rises from the broken bottle. A sickeningly sweet aroma fills my throat and lungs.

"Oh my gosh!" Kara whispers. She's far enough away to avoid the Essence of Infatuary. Her eyes latch on to me with shock and confusion. "Fred, what is this stuff?"

My throat is clogged with the potion. Like cake frosting in liquid form. A dreamy, light-headed fogginess comes over me. My head feels like a balloon that might float away any second. My vision turns a dazzling shade of pink. . . .

I blink. And when my gaze falls upon Kara again, a sudden realization sweeps over me.

Kara Estrada is the most beautiful girl I've ever seen.

Kara

Our lives are in danger. We're trapped in a twisted fantasy mall, surrounded by evil fairies and armored soldiers, but Prince Fred doesn't seem worried at all. In fact, the only thing he seems interested in is . . .

Me.

Fred can't take his eyes off me. A faint smile hangs from his face. He clutches his hands over his heart. He bats his eyelashes a few times and breathes a long, heavy sigh.

"Uh . . . Fred?" I whisper. "Everything okay?"

"Everything is *better* than okay," he replies. "Everything is *wonderful*, for I am with you!"

Still staring at me with that goofy grin, Fred scoots sideways until he's right next to me. He leans forward, bringing his face way too close to mine. His eyes flutter closed. His lips pucker.

He's coming in for a kiss.

I push him away. "What're you doing?"

Fred grabs my hand. But it's not like the way he grabbed my hand before. This time, it's desperate, clinging.

"I'm merely following my heart," he says. "When in the presence of such beauty and charm, I'm left with no choice. I must show my affection!"

Okay, so either Fred just picked the worst possible time to tell me about his crush, or the potion has kicked in. And I'm guessing Essence of Infatuary is some kind of love potion.

I've always been shy around boys. I guess I'm nervous they won't like me back. Whenever Marcy talks about the guys she likes, I always go quiet. That seems easier than the awkwardness of mentioning I've never had a boyfriend.

The only reason I'm confessing all this is to let you know that I don't have a ton of experience (okay, fine— *zero* experience) with boys telling me how much they like me.

And now—out of nowhere—I've got an actual fairy-tale prince saying how beautiful and charming I am? Part of me is like, *I wish Marcy could be here to see this.*

But none of the things Fred's saying is genuine. It's the potion talking. Besides, this is just about the *worst* time for romance. Ever since the bottle crashed, the clanging footsteps have stopped. The armored soldiers must've heard the disturbance. And now they're on alert.

Meanwhile, Prince Fred is still gripping my hand and staring deeply into my eyes.

"Your hair." He sighs. "It's so smooth and silky. And your nose." Another sigh. "How have I not yet noticed how adorable your nose is? And I mustn't overlook your chin. Oh, what an attractive chin you have!"

"Listen, Fred." I pull my hand out of his. "I appreciate the compliments, but now's not really the best time."

"But this cannot wait, Kara. I cannot bear to keep it in any longer—"

"Not now!" I hiss.

Fred stands up straight. At this point, he isn't even *trying* to hide. Spreading his arms, he looks up at the ceiling and calls out in a way-too-loud voice, "I'm in love with Kara Estrada, and I want the entire world to—"

I clamp my hand over Fred's mouth so that the rest of his announcement is muffled. For a second, everything's totally silent. Then I hear it.

The sound of clanging metal boots. And they're headed our way.

"We have to get out of here!" I say.

Fred nods. "Perhaps a candlelit restaurant? Someplace where we can snuggle up?"

"I'm not talking about a *date*!" I look out the doorway of the Potion Emporium. The clanking is getting louder and louder. "Hear that noise? That's the sound of armored soldiers. They're coming here to attack us."

"How unromantic!"

"And if we don't get out of here now, then we'll . . . uh— never get to go on a date."

"In that case, let us leave this place at once!"

We hurry out of the store. As soon as we pass through the doorway, my heart jumps into my throat. To the left, three soldiers are running toward us. Their silver visors are pulled down over their faces. Their swords are drawn. Their movements are perfectly in sync. Arms and legs rising and falling with an exactly timed rhythm, as if they choreographed their attack.

We race away from the soldiers. The sounds of their clattering armor seem to get louder and louder with each passing heartbeat.

"You look so attractive when you're running," Fred says between heaving breaths. "Your cheeks have a rosy flush and your brown eyes glitter with—"

"Not now!" I snap.

I scan the mall for a way out, but everything's a blur. I'm sure that—any second—I'll feel a heavy gauntlet come down on my shoulder. Then I see something. Up ahead, a passageway that leads to bathrooms and water fountains and . . .

The emergency exit.

For about half a second, I let myself feel just a tiny bit hopeful that we might make it out of the mall alive. Then I notice the sounds of armor aren't just coming from behind us. I can also hear rhythmic clattering in front of us.

Suddenly, three more armored soldiers come bursting out of the passageway. Their swords are drawn. Maybe they've been patrolling the bathrooms, because one guy has toilet paper trailing from the back of his boot.

We're trapped. If we keep going, we'll run right into the soldiers ahead of us. But turning around will just send us in the direction of the dudes who're chasing us.

That leaves only one other option.

"In here!" I tug Fred sideways, into a sporting goods store. It's the kind of place where you buy gym socks and basketballs. At least, that's what it *used* to be. Ever since the Sorceress's renovations, the shelves are now filled with *medieval* athletic supplies. Instead of football jerseys, there's chain mail. And where the tennis rackets used to be, there's a rack of battle-axes.

"Why did you lead us *here*, darling? This isn't romantic at all." Fred gazes at me with a mushy expression. "I noticed a flower store nearby. Let me take you there. I'll buy you the loveliest bouquet of tulips you've ever seen."

How am I ever supposed to fight off the Sorceress's evil minions with Prince Lover-Boy hanging all over me? Unless . . .

"Uh . . . actually, honey-poo," I begin. "Wanna know what I find *really* super-duper romantic?"

"What is that, my jewel?"

I grab a spiked club off the wall and push it into Fred's hands. "Fighting soldiers."

Fred gives me a perplexed look. "You must be joking."

"Nope. Totally serious. And if you want to be my . . . uh, boyfriend, then you've got to show me how good you are at beating up those soldier guys."

Fred strikes a heroic stance. "Of course, my dear! If that's what you wish! I shall gladly protect you from these vile soldiers and win your heart through acts of valor!"

And before I can say anything else, Fred charges across the store. He reaches the open doorway at the exact moment the first group of soldiers arrives.

Fred swings the club like it's a baseball bat, landing a massive hit right in the stomach of the middle soldier. The impact leaves a huge dent in the armor, but the soldier doesn't seem hurt at all. He raises his sword. He's about to bring the blade down on Prince Fred's neck when I join the fight.

In my rush, I grab the first weapon I can find. A small hatchet. It isn't nearly as big or deadly as the battle-axes, but it's light enough for me to swing with full force at the soldier's arm. *SCHLINK!* The hatchet slices through steel armor. And suddenly, the soldier's hand . . .

Falls off.

I let out a surprised yelp and brace myself for the gruesome aftermath. Gushing blood, severed bones. But none of that happens. Because the suit of armor is hollow. There's nobody inside.

My memory flashes back to all the empty suits of armor that lined the walls of Legendtopia. The Sorceress must've cast her spell on them, too.

The hollow gauntlet clanks to the floor, still gripping the sword. But the soldier doesn't stop. It brings a metal boot down on my foot. Searing hot pain flashes up my leg. I stagger backward, arms flailing. With the hatchet in my hand, I'm lucky I don't cut off any of my own limbs.

Prince Fred glares at the suit of armor. "How dare you

assault my beloved Kara!" He raises the club over his shoulder. "I shall turn you into scrap metal for that!"

WHAM!

With a single swing, Prince Fred knocks the soldier's head all the way to the food court.

But even *that* isn't enough to stop it. The headless, handless suit of armor lurches in Fred's direction. A whirl of flashing steel, swinging and kicking. And it's not the only attacker. Two more soldiers are closing in on us.

Doing my best to ignore the pain pulsing in my foot, I grip the hatchet with both hands and charge. A sword swipes at my shoulder, but I manage to block it with the hatchet blade. With my next swing, I detach the leg of another soldier. The armor clatters sideways with a hollow *CLONK!*

"Have I ever mentioned how lovely you look swinging a hatchet?" Prince Fred remarks.

"Thanks." I slice an arm off the nearest soldier. "You're not doing so bad yourself."

The floor around us is littered with random pieces of armor. But the soldiers just keep coming. One of them is missing its legs. And still the top half of the armor won't give up. It scoots forward, metal arms swinging wildly. From the other side, a single metal foot hops in our direction, ready to kick anything that crosses its path.

But they're not alone in the fight. Another battalion is approaching, footsteps clanging like clockwork.

"We can't hold them off forever," I say. "We need to keep moving."

"You're absolutely correct." Prince Fred steps toward me. "Although first, perhaps we have time for a quick kiss."

He puckers up. I resist the urge to take a swing with the hatchet. *How long till this stupid potion wears off?*

I give Prince Lover-Boy a *back off* look. "Not now, Fred."

"Ooh, playing hard-to-get." The prince winks. "I like that."

The crash of armor is getting dangerously close. "Just follow me!"

"I shall follow you anywhere, my dearest beloved!"

We take off running. There are probably some warnings against running with a hatchet in your hand, but I don't dare let go. I have a feeling I'll need the weapon again soon.

"The exit!" Without slowing down, I point to the glass doors at the end of a department store. "That way!"

We're almost there when the doorway shatters. Glass rains down on the floor. An extra-large figure clomps forward. A blur of gray. Before I can change directions—before I can do *anything*—an enormous hand swings at me.

A voice—Prince Fred's voice—calls out.

"Kara! No!"

Everything spins. My feet are no longer on the ground. I'm hurled through space.

Until I collide with a clothes rack.

Images flash past me. Tangles of fabric. Red, blue, brown. ALL MEN'S TUNICS 20% OFF!

Then the floor rises up like a wave and smacks me in the face.

A galaxy of stars swirls through my brain. Glancing around dimly, I see that I landed inside the rack of tunics. The view flickers. I feel myself fading. Sinking deeper and deeper into unconsciousness.

Then a thought pulls at my mind. *Prince Fred. He's in danger.*

I need to help him. But where's my hatchet? I must've lost it somewhere around the time I took a one-way flight across the department store. Not that it matters much. My entire body feels like it's wrapped in a cocoon. Surrounded by a gauzy numbness. Unable to stand. Unable to move at all. Unable to do anything but listen to the nearby ogres.

"YOU TAKE THE PRINCE." The ogre's voice is grumbly and gruff. "I'LL EAT THE GIRL."

Eat the girl? I don't like the sound of that. Once again, I try to push myself off the floor, but it's impossible. I'm too weak.

A second ogre joins the conversation.

"NO TIME FOR SNACK," it says. "SORCERESS SAY WE SHOULD BRING THE PRINCE RIGHT AWAY."

"C'MON, PLEAAAAZZZE!" begs the first ogre. "CAN'T I JUST HAVE A QUICK BITE?"

"NO!"

The first ogre lets out an angry grunt. "YER NO FUN," it mutters.

It takes all my effort to open my eyes. Through the dim haze, I can just barely make out two enormous gray shapes. One of them reaches down and grabs something on the floor. A small human figure. Prince Fred. By the looks of it, he's been knocked out. The ogre slings the prince over his shoulder. Then it lumbers through the shattered doorway. The other ogre casts a hungry glance back in my direction. It lets out a long sigh then follows its companion out the door.

The lights fade again, and everything turns to black.

Prince Fred

⁓

I awake with a hammering headache and a strong feeling of regret. My memory of recent events is shrouded in fog. The last thing I remember clearly is the smashed bottle. Essence of Infatuary spilling all around me. Inhaling a pink cloud into my lungs. And then . . .

Oh no.

Oh, dear heavens, no!

The potion. *Love in a bottle.* I practically took a bath in the stuff! Perhaps that's why my brain feels like a mashed potato. And it might also explain why scraps of embarrassing moments have begun to drift through my memory.

I wince at each new recollection. Grasping at Kara's

hands like a lovesick baboon. *Oh, what an attractive chin you have!* (Did I actually say such a ridiculous thing?) Attempting to kiss her—on multiple occasions! Declaring my love for her.

She probably thinks I'm an absolute idiot!

I need to apologize! But where's Kara? And—come to think of it . . .

Where am I?

For the first time since waking up, I take a close look at my surroundings. I'm seated on the floor of a small stone room. To my right is a wooden door. Light gleams through a single narrow window. When I attempt to climb to my feet, I'm yanked backward with a metallic clatter. I glance down and my confusion turns to fear. Iron shackles are clasped around my wrists. I'm chained to the wall.

A new memory crashes through my mind. Being chased through the mall by empty suits of armor. Approaching a glass doorway. Almost there. Almost. But then the glass shattered. And we were met by a gruesome duo of ogres. The first knocked Kara into a rack of tunics. I turned to help her, but the second ogre was already swinging its massive gray fist.

And the next thing I knew, I was here. In this room. Alone.

My unpleasant awakening is interrupted by a flutter of wings and the flicker of shadow. A crow has just landed on the windowsill. Its feathers are dark as midnight, and so are its eyes. Gleaming black pearls that peer in my direction. The bird opens its beak and lets out a shrill *CAWWW! CAWWW! CAWWW!* I could swear the thing is laughing at me.

The next time its beak parts, words come out.

"Did you enjoy your nap?" The crow casts a mocking glance around my prison cell. "How do you like your new room? Perhaps not the kind of thing you're used to, Mr. Fancy Prince? No more snooty servants to fluff your pillows and cook your meals? Well, you better *get* used to it. There's a new boss in town, and she's making some changes."

All of a sudden, I feel a strong urge to strangle the revolting bird. I pull at my shackles with all my might. The chains rattle and shake, but the effort does nothing to loosen my restraints.

The crow lets out another caw of laughter. Pointing its sharp black beak at my iron manacles, it says, "I like the new jewelry. Suitable for a prince such as yourself."

It's bad enough that I'm being held prisoner. But do I really need this horrid bird as my cell mate? Although . . .

perhaps the company of the crow isn't *all* bad. It could be a way to find out more information.

With a sigh, I drop back to the floor. Plopping my hands on my knees, I lock eyes with my feathery tormentor. "Well, then. Since you seem to know who I am, the least you can do is tell me your name."

The bird seems amused by my request. "I'll give you one guess."

"Very well. But if I get it right, you must answer another question. That's only fair."

After a moment's consideration, the crow nods. "Fine. What is your guess?"

I ponder the question. There are many possible names on Urth. But what about animals? My memory leaps back to our encounter with the frogs in Pevensie Park. Each had shared an identical name. A quite unoriginal name . . .

"Time's running out!" says the crow. "All contestants must provide their answers or lose out on their chance to win the grand prize. You have three seconds. Three . . . two . . ."

"Your name is Crow!"

I can tell by the crow's expression that I'm right. "How . . . ?" Its voice trembles with surprise. "How did you know?"

I glance down so it won't see my smirk. "Wild guess."

Crow flutters its wings, clearly impressed. In the over-loud voice of an announcer, it says, "Mr. Prince, you guessed correctly on the first try! You win the grand prize. An all-expenses-paid trip to an exclusive prison cell at the top of the tallest turret in Legendtopia!"

So I'm at the top of the tallest turret. That bit of infor-mation might be helpful later . . . *if* I ever manage to free myself from these accursed chains.

"That wasn't the only prize," I point out. "You also owe me the answer to one question."

Crow's black eyes gleam with annoyance. "Of course. Your question. Go ahead, then. Make it count."

This time, I don't need to think before speaking. The question comes at once. "Where is Kara?"

Is it my imagination, or did a smile form on Crow's beak? "Aww! Mr. Prince wants to check on his girlfriend! How sweet!"

"She's not my girlfriend!"

"That's funny. Back at the mall, you weren't too shy about your love for her."

Suddenly, my cheeks are burning. "That was the po-tion!"

"And yet, you still seem quite concerned. I can see it in

your face. This girl is more than a mere companion. I believe you have feelings for her."

"Nonsense! Now will you please—?"

Crow interrupts me in a teasing singsong voice. *"Mr. Prince and Kara, sitting in a tree! K-I-S-S-I-N—"*

"Answer the question!" I growl.

"Fine. I don't know where your girlfriend is."

Ignoring the "girlfriend" comment, I focus on the other thing Crow says. "What do you mean? What happened to her?"

Crow shrugs, a slight rise of black wings. "I already told you. I don't know. Last I heard, she escaped the mall. Nobody knows what happened to her after that."

I take a relieved breath. Kara made it out. She's safe. At least for now.

Crow must notice my reaction. He taps his beak against the stone windowsill. The sharp noise echoes through my cell like the final nail sinking into a coffin.

"It's only a matter of time till we find her," says the bird. "The Sorceress's army is growing stronger with every moment. Her minions are searching the village. Your girlfriend won't last long on her own. Most likely, she's already been captured. Or she's dead."

Crow's words hang over me, heavy and cold. The iron

shackles dig into my wrists. A terrible sense of dread sinks into my thoughts. And yet I refuse to give up hope. Kara may be young, and she may be alone, but she's many other things as well. She's intelligent, and resourceful, and strong.

She's the most courageous girl—no, *person*—I have ever met.

I'm about to say this to Crow when a sound catches my attention. A rattle at the door. The brass knob slowly begins to turn.

Crow's black eyes gleam with wicked excitement. "Looks like you have another visitor."

With a flutter of dark feathers, the bird flaps away from the window, cawing with laughter. A moment later, the door creaks open.

And in walks the Sorceress.

Kara

‒

I have no idea how long I was lying unconscious in the department store. All I know is, when I wake up, the ogres are gone. And so is Prince Fred.

At least the Sorceress demanded they take him alive. By now, he's probably being held prisoner somewhere in Legendtopia. So that means all I need to do is escape this department store, make it through the fantasy nightmare of Shady Pines, break into an enchanted castle, and find the prince.

Easy, right?

Making as little noise as possible, I climb to a sitting position. My head throbs. A dull pain clings to my foot. But at least the ogre knocked me into a clothes rack. Which means I'm surrounded by heavy brown tunics on clothes hangers. Kind of like being inside my own personal tent. It isn't exactly the best hiding spot, but at least it gives me some cover.

Through a slim gap in the tunics, I peer out at my surroundings. The door is a scene of destruction. Piles of bricks and shattered glass where the ogres made their entrance. The opening is being guarded by two suits of armor. One is missing a head, but they both have swords. And without a weapon of my own, I'm not about to take them on.

More soldiers are patrolling the store, joined by a few dozen fairies. They buzz from place to place. When I notice a couple heading in my direction, I huddle deep inside the clothes rack. I can hear their high-pitched chatter getting louder and louder.

"... *ogrrre says theeee girl is herrrre sssssomewherrre.*"

"*Whaaaat does she looook liiike?*"

"*She is exxxxtremely talllll.*"

"*All humans loooook exxxxtremely tallll to us, stuuupid.*"

"*Goooood point.*"

"*Whaaaat color hairrrr doessss the girl haaaave?*"

"*Brown.*"

"And whaaaat is she wearrrrring?"

"A whiiiite T-shirrrrt and bluuuuue jeans with graaaay sneakerrrrs."

I look down at my outfit. It's a perfect description. With so many minions patrolling the store, they're sure to find me eventually. And when they do, I won't stand a chance of convincing them I'm someone else.

Unless I find a disguise.

Once the fairies buzz off, I begin checking the labels of the tunics all around me. L . . . XL . . . XXL. The sizes are way too big for me. And besides, the brown wool feels super-itchy. It'd be like wearing a giant potato sack filled with mosquitoes. No thanks.

I take another peek outside. Not too far away is another rack of clothes. Swirls of pink and gold and blue. Flowery ribbons and curls of lace. The sign above the rack reads: CHILDREN'S BALL GOWNS—PERFECT FOR ANY SPECIAL OCCASION!!!

The colorful, puffy dresses aren't my style. But I don't have many other options.

When I'm sure the coast is clear, I make a run for the ball gowns.

I plunge inside the rack.

There's no easy way to be sneaky when you're trying on

a fluffy ball gown inside a tiny, confined space. The satin material swishes noisily. My fingers shake as I untie the knotted silk ribbons. I'm terrified that any second, a suit of armor will bust in on me in my underwear.

Once I'm through, I look down at my new outfit. A pastel-pink gown, lined with white lace and flowery bundles of silk. A wire hoop at the bottom causes the whole thing to bulge out around my legs.

How am I ever supposed to fight an evil witch and rescue a hostage prince while wearing *this*?

And I'm not even done playing dress-up. The Sorceress's minions also know that I have brown hair and gray shoes. I need to change that.

Along the wall is a shelf that used to hold baseball caps. Now it's displaying powdered wigs. The kind of fluffy white hair you see on French royalty in old paintings. I pluck one off the shelf. A massive, curly bundle of white hair. Trying the thing on, I feel like I'm wearing a bag of marshmallows on my head.

But, hey—at least my hair isn't brown anymore.

Now I just need a new pair of shoes. But as I'm on my way to the shoe section, my puffy dress knocks a stack of clothes hangers to the ground. The sound jangles across the store. A second later, a high-pitched voice calls out.

"You therrrre! Huuuuman! Stop riiight whhhere you arrrre!"

All the blood freezes in my veins. The flapping of the fairy's wings fills my ears, loud as a buzz saw. A second later, it appears in front of me. From up close, it looks even creepier. The thing's no bigger than my thumb. Glowing skin. Narrow golden eyes. Pointy teeth.

I'm definitely not dealing with Tinker Bell here.

The fairy looks me up and down suspiciously. It hovers around my powdered wig and circles my fancy ball gown.

"Whhhhat are you doinnng in heeeere, human?" it asks.

My brain spins to come up with a response.

"Welllll?" The fairy's accusing tone hits an even higher pitch than usual. *"Whhhhat do you havvvve to sayyyy? Speak, hummmman! Orrr else I shallll havvvve one of the soldiers chhhhop offfff your tongue."*

Every moment of hesitation feels like a lifetime. I think about making a run for it. But in a dress like this, I wouldn't make it ten feet. So I open my mouth. And I speak the first words that come to mind.

"My sole authority," I say in a dull, even tone. "My ruler. My queen."

I do my best to act brainwashed. Glazed eyes. Drooping mouth.

"My sole authority," I repeat. "My ruler. My—"

"*Yeah, yeah. Weeeee get iiiit.*" The fairy rolls its eyes. "*Humans cannnn be sooooo annoying. You shouldn't beee here, human. This mallll is parrrrt of the Sorceress's domainnnn.*"

"My sole authority," I say. "My—"

"*Just leaaaave!*" the fairy snaps, pointing a tiny glowing finger toward the exit.

I grab a pair of golden slippers on my way out.

⁓

That's how I end up wandering the streets of Shady Pines in a puffy satin gown that makes me look like a human wedding cake. The curly powdered wig keeps getting in my eyes. The golden slippers dig into my heels with every step.

Every muscle in my body wants to run, to race as quickly as possible to Legendtopia. Prince Fred's in trouble. No telling what horrible things the Sorceress is doing to him. But there are too many of her minions around. And they're all on the lookout for me. And so I do my best brainwashed zombie impression, lurching dull-eyed in the direction of the massive funnel cloud.

I hardly recognize my town any longer. Shady Pines has become a twisted fantasy theme park. I pass by a shopping center that looks more like a medieval village square. The stores transformed into thatch huts. Wooden signs advertising butter churns, blacksmiths, shoe cobbling. In the parking lot is a man whose hands and head are clasped inside a painful-looking wooden device. We learned about this kind of thing in social studies. *The stocks.* That's what they're called. A crowd is gathered around the man, taunting him, throwing rotten vegetables.

There's only one way to put an end to this madness. By stopping the Sorceress.

At the intersection, a yellow school bus is being pulled by a team of horses. It's like some kind of a weird, hybrid bus-carriage. The driver's seat is vacant, but that doesn't mean there isn't a driver. Sitting on the hood of the bus, with the reins in her hands, is Mrs. Olyphant. My English lit teacher.

I turn my stunned gaze to the rest of the bus. Through the windows, I can see my entire fourth-period class. Their eyes stare blankly ahead. Their expressions are empty. Twenty-something middle schoolers, chanting the same thing over and over again.

"My sole authority. My ruler. My queen."

Near the back of the bus, I spot the seat that's occupied by Trevor Fitzgerald. He doesn't look nearly so smug anymore. His mouth hangs open. A glob of spittle quivers from his bottom lip. One seat behind him is Marcy. Her eyes are glazed over. She keeps repeating the Sorceress's words mindlessly. Seeing my friend like this is heartbreaking. It used to be her dream to live in a fantasy world. Now it's become a nightmare.

I clench my hands into fists. An inferno of anger and determination swirls inside me. Someone needs to stop the Sorceress. To bring her cruel magic to an end. And that someone is *me*.

The horse-drawn school bus clatters in one direction. I go in the other. Until I finally approach the place that I've been trying to reach all day.

Legendtopia.

Worried that my disguise won't work so close to the Sorceress's evil headquarters, I crouch between a couple of parked cars. The gown bunches up around my waist. The curly, white wig falls into my eyes.

Legendtopia looks nothing like the place we visited yesterday. The cheesy fake-castle restaurant has been replaced by a massive stone fortress. Impenetrable dark gray walls. Towers and turrets rising high into the air. Yesterday, there was a shallow goldfish pond in front of the door. Now it's a moat. Whatever's swimming through the gloomy water is gold in color, but looks as big as a shark.

The enormous steel doors are closed. Guards patrol the perimeters.

I've got to figure out a way inside. The only question is . . . *how?*

Prince Fred

The Sorceress stands before me, hands clutched behind her back. Sunlight traces the lines of her beautiful, terrible features.

"So lovely to see you again, Prince Frederick," she says in a pleasant voice, as if she's invited me over for tea and cake. "How have you enjoyed your time on Urth so far?"

I scowl at her in furious silence. The corners of the Sorceress's lips curl into a smile.

"I quite like it, actually," she continues. "The people here have made me feel right at home."

"Because you brainwashed them!" I growl.

I only learned the word "brainwashed" a few hours ago

when Kara used it, but it seems the most fitting description of what the Sorceress is doing. Going inside people's brains. Washing away their personalities, their thoughts, *everything*. Turning them into her mindless slaves.

The Sorceress smiles down at me like a polite hostess, but her eyes . . .

Her eyes are dark and evil.

"Urth is full of such fascinating magic," she says in a delighted voice. "Of course, the people here call it 'technology,' but you and I"—she raises her eyebrow at me—"we know the truth. It *is* magic. Back in our world, if I wanted to cast an enchantment spell on someone, I had to be in the same room. I needed to look them in the eyes. But here . . . I can cast my spell through screens. And the best part is—there are screens everywhere! And the people of Urth always seem to be looking at them. It's perfect!"

As much as I hate to acknowledge it, the Sorceress has a point. I've seen the way people here constantly check their Self-Owns. The way Kneel spends hours playing his video games and exploring the Internet. The televisions flickering endlessly in the windows of homes.

And the Sorceress knows this, too. The best way into people's brains is through their screens.

"But the magic of technology doesn't stop there!" she

says. "They have such marvelous weaponry here on Urth. Things that make our swords and axes look like children's playthings. Weapons that can engulf entire nations in fiery destruction with the mere push of a button."

Although a warm light still glows in the window, I feel a bitter chill enter the room. I can't bear to listen to another word. Before the Sorceress can say anything else, I speak in a furious, trembling whisper.

"This scheme of yours will never succeed!" I say. "The armies of Urth will stop you!"

"The armies of Urth?" Amusement gleams in the Sorceress's dark eyes. "Soon the armies of Urth will *serve* me."

"Then what am I doing here?" I rattle at my chains. "If you're so powerful, then what do you need with me?"

"You are my ransom."

I heard the ogres use the exact same term earlier. "Ransom for what?"

The Sorceress narrows her black eyes. "You really *are* a brainless little worm. Do you not see the purpose you serve in all this?"

I ignore the insult. My entire concentration is elsewhere. "What purpose?"

"You are the son of the queen and king. The most powerful couple in all of Heldstone. They would grant me anything to have you back. Anything."

"You already have countless minions. What more can you possibly want?"

The Sorceress sighs. "My minions have served me well. But there is a limit to what they can do. Just look at the ogres. Sure, they're strong and obedient. But they're clumsy and dull-witted, too. The same goes for my armored soldiers. They might *look* fierce, but the truth is, they are little more than empty tin cans."

The Sorceress turns and gazes out the window longingly, as though imagining the day that she will rule every inch of Urth.

"What I need is a *real* army," she goes on. "A ruthless, efficient army. And I know just where to find one. . . ."

The Sorceress doesn't have to say any more. I already know precisely where she will get her army. From Heldstone. My parents will give it to her. And all she has to give them in exchange is her prisoner, her hostage, her ransom.

Me.

A dagger of fury twists inside me. The Royal Guard is the most experienced and loyal army in the history of Heldstone. Tens of thousands of them. Commanders, knights, soldiers. Bound by oath to obey the orders of the king and queen. My parents. Even if that means fighting on the side of the Sorceress.

"Once they discover that I'm keeping you captive in

Urth, your mommy and daddy will agree to march their entire army—one by one—through the miniature door," the Sorceress says. "All the might of Heldstone's greatest army *and* Urth's superior weaponry? All in the hands of the most powerful wizardess in history? Nothing will be able to stop me. *Nothing.*"

The Sorceress's expression is a mask of pure evil. Swirls and tangles of black hair, casting clawlike shadows over her icy features. Dark eyes of bottomless cruelty.

"Before long, I will rule all of Urth," she says. "But why stop there? Without their army, your mommy and daddy will be defenseless. Unable to fight against the power that I have assembled on Urth. At long last, all of Heldstone will fall to its knees and recognize me as their one true queen."

My thoughts plunge into a pit of fear. The Sorceress is on the verge of ruling both our worlds. And Kara is the only one who can stop her.

Kara

A horse-drawn police van is headed for Legendtopia. Hooves clomp the concrete. The van rattles closer. A uniformed officer is slumped on top. I worry that he'll see me. But he's too dazed by the Sorceress's spell to notice anything except the horses' butts in front of him.

This might be my only chance. I check one last time to make sure there aren't any monsters nearby. All clear. I bolt from my hiding spot.

My dress billows around me. The wig flops around on my head like a fluffy white octopus. I manage to make it to the van without being noticed. Lunging forward, I grab the handle to the back door and yank it open.

Pulling myself into the back of the van, I snag my dress on the bumper. I grasp to pull it loose at the same time that the van hits a pothole and—

RRRRIIIIIP!

I tumble backward into a heap of satin and ribbons. A huge gash runs down the bottom of my dress. It looks like I've been mauled by a tiger on my way to a fancy ball. But there's no time for fashion concerns. The van's nearing Legendtopia and the back door's still wide open.

I lunge forward and close the door just as we reach the moat. A muffled voice calls out from the roof.

"Munitions for Her Majesty!"

The van is crowded with metal crates. They rattle all around me. When I peek inside one of them, a chill seeps into my bones.

The crate's filled with guns. And so are most of the others. A few are carrying bullets or knives. Basically, I'm hiding out in a traveling arsenal.

The van jostles over the drawbridge. I'm entering the castle.

From a crate in the corner, I grab a knife with a serrated edge and go to work on my torn gown. I'm not much of a seamstress, but I can at least make it easier to sneak around by cutting away some of the puffier parts. I slash at satin, toss silk ribbons aside, chop lace to shreds.

When I'm finished, I'm surrounded by piles of torn fabric. My gown's been cut to the length of my knees. The bottom part is a jagged mess of uneven layers. Pink scraps hanging off everywhere. I think I just invented a whole new fashion. Fairy-tale punk.

The van lurches to a halt. Gripping the hilt of the knife even tighter, I listen to the sounds from outside the vehicle. Heavy, plodding footsteps. A guttural grunt. The handle rattles.

And suddenly, the back door swings open.

I find myself looking at the giant gray belly of an ogre. At its full height, the creature is too tall to see into the van. But when it hunches down, the ogre's shiny black eyes go wide with surprise.

Then the monster lunges at me. I stumble backward, tripping over a crate and landing hard on my back. With a groan, I raise my head. And that's when I see the ogre coming in for a belly flop right on top of me.

I clench my eyes shut, expecting the worst. I'm about to be crushed. Or eaten. Or both. But none of that happens. And when I open my eyes again, I find the ogre lying beside me. Unmoving. And the knife that was in my hand—the knife I used to alter my dress . . .

It's now buried in the monster's chest.

The ogre undergoes a strange transformation right in

front of me. Its eyes turn into dull glass. Its thick skin softens into plain gray fabric. The thing's body begins to shrink—from a ten-foot monster into something that's barely bigger than me.

The ogre has gone back to its old form. An oversized stuffed animal with cotton poking out of its seams and loose wiring in its ears.

Poking my head out of the van, I cast a shaky glance in both directions. The inside of the castle is a hive of activity. Ogres stacking crates of guns. Armored guards assembling new foot soldiers out of scrap metal. Weird creations just waiting to be turned evil by the Sorceress.

Near the center of the room is a long wooden table of computers. Wires snake past tablets and laptops. A group of fairies looks to be in charge of the digital command center. They tap keyboards and survey Google Maps, hissing high-pitched orders into phones that are twice their size.

Luckily, the minions are all too busy with their tasks to notice me. I creep across the chamber, keeping close to the wall. Past a couple of flaming torches and a leering stone gargoyle. I take cover behind a velvet curtain when I catch an extremely unwelcome sight.

The Sorceress.

She's even more beautiful and more horrible than I

remember. She drifts down the stairs, her black dress trailing behind her.

She points a pale finger at a suit of armor. "Go to the kitchen and fetch some food for the prince. We must keep him alive. At least until we get what we want from his parents."

The guard nods and clanks away. Five minutes later it returns with a tray of food. The armor starts up the stairs. I follow it.

The stairway twists up and up and up. I trail the metallic footsteps higher into the shadowy tower.

When the clanging steps come to a stop, I pause next to a narrow window and peer around the corner. The guard stoops in front of a locked door, jangling a set of keys. My eyes land on one key in particular. A huge golden key that's much larger than all the others. It dangles from the brass ring, gleaming in the dim light.

I wonder what lock *that* opens.

All of a sudden, a sound of flapping wings jostles my attention. Whirling around, I spot a bird coming in for a landing on the windowsill.

A crow.

The black bird opens its beak and lets out a series of caws that sound a whole lot like it's laughing at me. I flick a hand in its direction, hoping to shoo it away, but the crow won't budge. Instead, it watches me with a gleam of amusement in its dark eyes. And the next time it opens its beak, the thing speaks.

"Well, well," it says in a harsh voice. "Did you come to visit Mr. Prince? You know, he asked about you. Too bad you won't live to see him."

I take another swing, but the crow jabs at my hand with its sharp beak. Then it flaps into the stairway, its loud cries echoing throughout the tower.

"There's an intruder in the castle! An intruder trying to take our hostage!"

So much for the element of surprise.

The guard above me is the first to respond. It drops the set of keys and rushes in my direction. Its banging armor sounds like a washing machine falling down the stairs. *CLANG! SQUINK! BONK!* And suddenly, it's directly above me.

Right about now, I could really use the knife. But I stupidly left it back in the police van, buried in the ogre's chest. And so all I can do is stumble backward as the guard raises its sword. I scramble down another step and the long blade smacks the stone wall where I just was. Sparks fly. The guard makes another lunge. This time, I duck and the sword clashes with the wall above me.

The only thing keeping me alive is the confined spiral staircase. The guard's armor is too bulky. Its sword is too long. It can't maneuver enough to take a clean swipe at me. It clatters after me, stomping and slashing. But I'm smaller. I can move more easily. Crouching and scuttling, I'm able to dodge the guard's attacks.

Then I hear the sound of other footsteps. Something enormous is clomping up the stairs.

I whirl sideways just in time to see another ogre. Its massive body takes up the entire stairway. With a deafening growl, the creature takes a swing. I flatten myself against the wall. Its humongous gray fist blurs right past me and instead slams into the guard. The armor explodes into a dozen pieces.

The ogre bellows with rage. "RRAAARRR! LITTLE GIRL TRICKED ME! YOU'LL PAY FER THAT!"

Before the creature can begin its next attack, I bolt up the steps. The stairway behind me is an echo chamber of terrifying noises. Giant feet pummeling stone, furious roars. It sounds like an entire army of monsters is behind me.

It doesn't take long to reach the top of the stairway. The only escape is the wooden door. But that's closed—and locked.

The keys that the guard dropped are still lying on the

floor. I grab them, but there are too many. I'll never find the right key in time. I glance up at the exact moment that the ogre lunges for me. But in the tight stairway, the monster's even clumsier than usual. Its foot snags the top step. It tumbles forward, and—

KA-BLAAAM!

Looks like I won't need the key after all. The door shatters and the ogre plunges into Prince Fred's room like a wrecking ball.

Prince Fred

Growing up in the Royal Palace, I often imagined situations like this. A hostage, kept captive in the enemy's tower. A valiant hero storming the castle. In my imagination, of course, *I* was always the hero. The brave prince who rescues the damsel in distress. Now the scenario has finally come to life.

Except *I'm* the one being rescued.

A tremor jolts the turret. The wooden door bursts apart and an ogre comes barreling into the room.

The monster appears surprised. As if it had not planned on breaking through the door at all. A second later, its dark eyes land upon me and its features shift into a more familiar expression.

Uh-oh. Now the ogre looks hungry.

My insides twist into a knot of fear. It's never a pleasant experience to be trapped inside a very small room with a very large ogre. But it's considerably worse when the ogre is looking at you like you're its lunch.

"SNACK TIME!" says the ogre. "I'M STARVING!"

My shackles rattle behind me. "You *can't* eat me," I remind the ogre. "I'm a hostage. The Sorceress wants me alive."

"JUST ONE LEG. SHE PROB'LY WON'T EVEN NOTICE."

"I promise you—she will!"

But the ogre ignores my plea. It lumbers forward, slobber dripping down its chin. I scramble backward, chains clattering, until my back is pressed against the wall. There's nowhere else to go.

The monster grasps my ankle with its enormous gray hand. I flail and kick, but the ogre's grip only tightens. Gritting my teeth, I await the jolt of pain. But it never comes. Instead, a pink blur bolts across the room.

I can't believe my eyes. It's Kara. Wearing a pink ball gown that's been roughly slashed apart at the knees. On her head is a crooked white wig. And in her hands—a sword. A glint of silver as she raises the weapon above her head . . .

And then plunges it into the ogre's back.

The monster releases its grip on my leg and collapses to the floor. But its death scene is more of a transformation. The ogre's entire body shrinks, becoming what it was before. A lifeless piece of decoration with gray cloth for skin and glass beads for eyes. Nothing more.

I glance up at Kara. "I certainly am glad to see you again!"

"Me too," she says. "Are you okay?"

"For the most part. Except for being chained to the wall."

"I might have something for that!" Kara lifts a brass key ring. One of the many keys is much larger than the rest. A golden key that's nearly as long as my hand. Far too big to unlock my restraint. I can only hope one of the others does the trick.

"Where did you get those?" I inquire.

"Guard dropped them outside your door."

The keys jingle as Kara crosses the room. She hunches beside me to try out one of the keys. There's a heavy clank of metal against metal. Wrong key. And there are at least a dozen more on the ring, not counting the oversized golden key.

As Kara tries out one after the other, I cast a curious look at her strange clothing. From the waist up, she looks ready for a fancy ball. Pink satin, fine lace, silken ribbons. But the bottom of the dress is another story. Someone has altered the gown in a most brutal fashion. And her wig? It sits lopsidedly on her head. Tufts of her brown hair poke out the sides.

"Might I ask . . . ," I begin. "How'd you end up dressed like that?"

Kara tries to jam another key into the lock—without success. "I changed outfits on the way over. Then I did a little redesign in the back of a police van."

"Police van?"

"It's kind of a long story. If we survive this, I'll tell you all about it."

My eyes land on the ogre—or what's left of it, anyway. The silver blade stands at an angle from its back. "Where'd you get the sword?"

"One of the guards tried to attack me with it. Right before it got punched by Mr. Ogre. I grabbed it off the stairs. And I'm guessing I got here just in time. That ogre was about to treat your leg like a basket of chicken wings."

I have at least a thousand more questions, but they'll have to wait. A great commotion echoes beyond the shattered door. It sounds as if an entire army is rushing up the stairs.

I turn a nervous glance back in Kara's direction. "If you could hurry it up with that lock, I would most appreciate it."

"I'm going as fast as I can." She rattles one key, then the next, muttering to herself, "Please, please, pl—"

CLICK!

The restraints around my wrists loosen. As I rise to a standing position, the chains clank to the floor. A rush of relief floods me. So this is what the damsel in distress feels like when she's rescued by the dashing knight.

It's not the way I imagined this situation playing out, but I'll take it.

"We need to get to the stairway," Kara says. "It's a tight space. They'll only be able to attack us one at a time."

Every instinct in my body resists the thought of running *toward* the enemies. Not when we're so badly outnumbered. But Kara's right. If we wait in the turret, we'll be ambushed in seconds. Within a cramped spiral staircase, on the other hand—well . . .

Our chances of survival are still pretty grim. But at least they're *slightly* better.

Kara glances at the sword in the ogre's back. "Do you want to—?"

"You take it," I say quickly. "You clearly know how to use the thing."

There's no time for argument. Kara grabs the sword and I follow her to the stairs. A few steps down, we pass a scattered heap of armor. The remains of the guard that attacked her on the way up. I reach down and grab a silver breastplate. I have a feeling the broad steel piece might prove useful soon enough.

We twist down several more steps. Terrifying sounds thunder in the confined space. Pounding footsteps, crashing armor, furious roars. But we keep moving. Forward. Down. Our only way to escape.

We don't stop until the first of them appears below us. I exchange a steady glance with Kara. Then we prepare for battle.

Kara

An entire horde of magical monsters is waiting patiently in a single-file line just to attack us.

If they get to Prince Fred, maybe they'll take him captive again. But in my case, they won't go to all that trouble. They'll just kill me.

The first one we meet is a guard. The suit of armor lunges with its sword. A deadly glint of silver. I flatten myself against the wall and the blade sparks against stone. Before it can recover, I take a swing at its head.

SHIIINK!

The guard's metal helmet pops off its shoulders and bounces down the steps like a volleyball. But that doesn't stop the fight. The headless suit of armor thrusts the sword again. I'm off balance, unable to defend myself. Luckily, Prince Fred is there. Before the sword reaches me, he dives between us. He's gripping a big silver chunk of armor. The guard's sword clanks against the armor like a shield.

Fred's next move comes a split second later. He bashes the steel plate against the guard's arm, knocking its sword loose—with its arm still attached. I chop off the guard's legs with two quick slices.

The guard—*or what's left of it*—collapses to the ground. But there are plenty more where that came from.

Fred and I are preparing our next attack when the dim stairway turns into a light show. A flurry of glowing orbs bounces through the air, casting crazy shadows against the stone walls. It takes another moment for my brain to catch up with what I'm seeing.

Fairies.

The winged creatures are small enough to cut to the front of the line. They buzz around us like evil humming-birds. Kicking, pulling, poking. And that's not all. The crow has joined the battle. The same crow that alerted the whole castle that I'm here. It must've flapped in through the window. Black wings flailing, sharp beak stabbing.

All of a sudden, the fight's coming at us from both

directions. I'm faced with the guards in front of us. And Fred has no choice but to hold off the fairies and the crow behind us. He swings his armor like a giant metal fly-swatter, smacking a fairy into the wall.

As soon as it hits the floor, the fairy undergoes the same change that happened to the ogres: from living creature to cheap restaurant decoration. The fairy's glow fades to nothing. Its skin transforms into hard papier-mâché.

But there are more. Lots of them. The crow and the fairies from one side, the guards from the other. I manage to dismantle a few more suits of armor. But when I see my newest opponent, a shocked breath escapes my lungs.

It's some kind of . . . mutant minion.

The thing's about the size of a guard, and moves with the same clunky gestures. But that's where the compari-sons end. Instead of armor, this dude's made out of stuff you'd find at the landfill. A broken microwave for a head. Torso made out of a spare tire. Arms and legs composed of rusty pipes.

If it doesn't bash my head in, I'll at least need a tetanus shot.

I saw creations like this down in the main hall. Scraps of metal and junky appliances, stitched together into humanlike forms that would make Dr. Frankenstein proud. Seeing them now is like a window into the Sorceress's evil plan. The stuff she found in Legendtopia—the ogres and armor and fairies . . . that's only the beginning. Her ambitions are much bigger than that. And to make them a reality, she's bringing in reinforcements from outside. Piles of junk and broken technology. Anything that can be scrapped together to expand her minion army. All with the goal of taking over the world.

And now, here they are. The first wave of mutant minions.

I lunge with the sword. The blade embeds deep inside the minion's spare tire stomach. The monster twists, yanking the sword's hilt out of my hands. I grasp for my weapon. Instead, I get smacked by a steel pipe.

Pain blazes through half my body. I duck just in time to avoid the next assault. A metallic crash explodes by my ear. Scrambling on the steps, I nearly trip over scraps of armor. The stairway is littered with the dismantled remains of the guards we've already fought. I grab the first thing I can get my hands on. A steel boot. Swinging, I slam the minion with all my strength.

WHAM! Right in its stupid microwave face.

With another hit, I knock the thing's head off. It stumbles backward. When I notice it teetering on the edge of a step, I kick the minion in its spare tire belly. This sends it tumbling down the stairs, crashing into the line of other mutant minions beneath it.

It's like watching a junk pile fight itself. Old television sets crashing into toaster ovens, lawn mower parts smacking fax machines. The devastation clears a path down the twisting stairway.

"Nice work!" Prince Fred calls to me from a few steps up.

It looks like he's taken care of his share of enemies, too. Papier-mâché fairies are littered around his feet. The crow flaps away, whimpering in pain.

Fred points down the steps. "We should make haste. Before they recover."

I drop the boot and grab a better weapon. A sword. Prince Fred grips a sword of his own in one hand, with the steel shield in his other.

"Let's go!"

We scramble down the spiraling stairs until we reach a door. I twist the handle. Locked. Good thing I still have the set of keys. The huge golden key glimmers in the dim stairwell. Just looking at it, I can tell it's way too big for the lock. And so I try the rest, one after the other. On the fourth attempt, the handle turns and the door swings open.

We rush inside. I use the same key to lock the door behind us. The lock slides into place just as the mutant minions clatter back up the stairway on the other side of the door.

Prince Fred and I turn. For the first time, I look across the room we just entered.

We've made a terrible mistake.

Prince Fred

We're inside a massive chamber, looking down from a second-story balcony. A set of stairs descends below us. The vaulted ceiling soars far above, held aloft by dark, twisted columns. Flickering torches line the walls. In one corner dozens of boxes are stacked atop one another, each stamped with the same large letters:

HANDLE WITH CAUTION
HIGHLY EXPLOSIVE

But it's what I see at the other end of the room that stops me cold.

The dragon.

It's the same monstrous creature that we encountered yesterday. The lump of fabric that the Sorceress transformed into a scale-covered, fire-breathing dragon. Except the beast has grown quite a bit since then. Even curled up on the floor, it's taller and longer than Kara's house. A row of huge, pointed talons poke out from beneath the dragon's leathery wings. I shiver to imagine the destruction it could wreak.

The creature's eyes are closed. The sound of its snoring is thunderous. It lets out a particularly loud grunt and a burst of flames spurts from its jaws.

The dragon is deadly even in its sleep.

A thick iron shackle has been clasped around one of the dragon's legs. Nearby is an enormous bowl for food and an equally large bowl for water. Both empty.

I can't believe it. The dragon is being kept like the world's biggest guard dog.

And that's when I notice what it's guarding. Behind the curled, sleeping form of the dragon is a broad silver box.

I gasp. It's the walk-in refrigerator.

The portal to Heldstone.

The doorway to my world.

As I look upon it, an idea glimmers in my mind like a

jewel. If we can get to the refrigerator, we'll be able to return to Heldstone and warn my parents, tell them about
the Sorceress's scheme. They can then muster their army
and seize the castle *from the inside*. We can stop the Sorceress before she gains any more power on Urth.

I whisper my plan to Kara. The more I dwell on it, the
more excited I become. "If we succeed, the bards will sing
my praises! The tales of my bravery will last for thousands
of years! I bet there'll even be a parade, with carnival per-
formers and a band and—"

Kara jabs me in the side. "Don't you think you're getting
just a little bit ahead of yourself?"

"Sorry." I tilt a glance in Kara's direction. "Would you
like a parade as well?"

"I don't want a *parade*! Right now, all I care about is getting past that dragon."

From a distance, I examine the broad, silver door of the
walk-in refrigerator. A chain is looped through the handle. And at the other end of the chain is the dragon.

My legs tremble. The terrible logic of our situation
dawns on me. There is only one way to unlock the door.

We'll have to release the dragon.

It's our only choice. The dragon's not merely guarding the door. It's *attached* to the door. In the center of the

beast's shackle is a huge golden keyhole. Which looks exactly the right size for the huge golden key in Kara's hand.

Now we just need to get close enough to unlock the dragon. Preferably *without* being burned to a crisp or eaten alive.

"Let's go," I whisper. "While it's still sleeping."

I push open the iron gate at the bottom of the steps. The hinges release a loud *SQUEEEEK!*

The dragon's eyes lazily open. It yawns, showing off a horrifying row of sharp teeth. From its mouth comes a puff of fire. As the beast's glance darts around the room, Kara and I hide behind a stone pillar.

Kara groans. "I liked the dragon a whole lot more when it was a puppet."

I peek around the edge of the pillar. The iron shackle around the dragon's leg is covered in deep grooves and scratches. The dragon's leg is equally damaged. Dark blood seeps from a wound.

"The dragon wants out of here," I say.

"That makes two of us," Kara mutters.

"It's been gnawing at its restraints. And even its own leg. It doesn't care about guarding the refrigerator. All it wants is—"

"Escape," Kara says. "The thing spends all its time locked in this windowless room. Chained to the floor."

"No telling how long since it's been fed. The poor creature is probably starving."

"Which means the *poor creature* will eat us the first chance it gets," Kara points out.

"Unless we offer it other food."

Kara knits her brow. "What do you mean?"

I point across the vast room. Another walk-in refrigerator. It looks similar to the one we entered Urth through—only newer. Probably a remnant of what this room once was. A kitchen.

"Walk-in refrigerators are ordinarily used to keep food cold, right?" I say.

Kara nods. "At least when they don't function as magical portals to other worlds."

"Then perhaps that's where they keep the dragon's food."

"Okay? And?"

"Maybe we can distract it. By giving it food."

"And what happens if the dragon comes after us?" she asks. "Once it isn't chained to the door, there's nothing to stop it."

"You said yourself. All it wants is escape. We're giving it

that. Plus a great quantity of food. It may even be grateful toward us."

"Oh, sure." Kara rolls her eyes. "I bet it'll write us a thank-you letter—right before it barbecues us."

"What does *barbecue* mean?"

"Doesn't matter. The point is, your plan's completely bonkers!"

I don't know what the word "bonkers" means, either, but I can guess its definition from the look on Kara's face. *Foolish. Unwise. Utterly crazy.* And worst of all—I know she's correct.

But what other options do we have?

In the end, a bonkers plan is better than no plan at all.

Kara

When the dragon's looking the other way, Fred and I sneak to the next pillar. We reach it just as the creature's head swivels back in our direction. Then we wait.

Glancing to one side, I notice the boxes in the corner. There must be at least fifty, stacked in orderly rows far beyond the dragon's fiery breath. And each includes stenciled words that read:

HANDLE WITH CAUTION
HIGHLY EXPLOSIVE

More of the Sorceress's stockpiled weapons. My spine tingles with horror. No telling what kind of destruction she could cause with that many explosives. Probably enough to wipe Shady Pines off the map.

My dark thoughts are interrupted by a sound. Clanging footsteps. An instant later, two mutant minions clank into the room. One has a mini-fridge torso, with a computer monitor for a head and copper tubes for arms and legs. The other's body is made up of a filing cabinet, chain saws, and an old copy machine.

The Sorceress sure has a strange idea of recycling.

The mutant minions probably saw us enter this room earlier. And now they're searching for us. I press my back against the pillar, my heartbeat loud in my ears. The dragon is scary enough. The last thing we need is *more* enemies.

The clatter of footsteps echoes through the room. It sounds like the minions are getting closer. Peeking around the pillar, I catch sight of them. And they're looking right at me. The minions set out at a run, their junkyard legs banging the tile. But before they reach us, the dragon lashes forward as far as its chain allows. Its mouth opens wide and a wave of flames bursts out. Within seconds, the minions are reduced to a pile of melted plastic and charred metal.

As I watch the scene, all I can think is *We could be next.*

Prince Fred tugs at my elbow. "Come on! While it's still distracted!"

We race the rest of the way to the walk-in fridge. Fred opens the door and I bolt inside. He joins me an instant later.

"I see what you mean about refrigerators being cold." He shivers, hugging his arms in front of his chest. "It's chillier in here than a Northlands blizzard. But where's the ice?"

"There is no ice," I say.

"But how do they keep it so cold? Wait—don't tell me!" Fred looks like he's trying to remember a vocab word that he studied last night. Then his eyes light up. "I remember! Eplextribily!"

"You mean *electricity*. And yes—that's why it's so cold. Now let's get the meat."

In the center of the walk-in refrigerator is a cart, stacked high with huge hunks of raw meat. The heap must weigh a couple hundred pounds. It takes both of us to push the cart through the door and back into the chamber.

Every step brings us closer to the dragon. I know I ought to be terrified. The thing's as big as a two-story house. Its golden eyes gleam with hunger. But as we approach, all I feel is sympathy. The dragon's a prisoner in the castle.

Locked away all by itself. Ignored, neglected, starving. Desperately biting at the shackle. Blood trickling down its leg and pooling around its claws.

The dragon has just as much reason to hate the Sorceress as we do.

The cart squeaks. We're close enough now for the dragon to reach us with its fiery breath. My memory keeps flashing with the horrifying image of what happened the last time anyone was this close to the dragon. Bursting flames, melting minions.

I really don't want to end up like that.

But even though the enormous creature could totally incinerate us right now, it doesn't. Somewhere in its dragon brain, it must know that killing us would be a stupid idea. *Roast the humans = no food.* The thing nudges its giant bowl with its snout and paws eagerly at the ground, like a dog on a leash, waiting to be fed.

I grip the handle tighter. Sweat drips down my forehead.

When we're close enough, Fred and I exchange a look.

"You ready?" I ask.

He nods. "We'll need to move quickly. Do you have the key?"

I raise the key ring, the huge golden key gripped in my palm. "On the count of three, we push."

Fred takes a deep breath. "One."

My voice trembles as I speak. "Two."

And together we say, "Three."

Push.

The cart rolls across the floor. The dragon surges forward. With a single flap of its wings, the creature lifts off the ground. For a moment, I get a glimpse of its full size and fury. Glistening teeth, lashing tail, wings spread wide, claws extended. The monster is even bigger than I'd realized. And scarier.

The dragon pounces on the meat. There's no telling how long it'll take to devour the entire cart. But one thing's for sure. Fred and I don't want to stick around long enough to become the second course.

We race toward the dragon, careful to approach from behind. It takes all my nerve to keep moving. Past the thing's long, flicking tail. Listening to the sickening crunch and smack of its eating.

Nearer, and nearer, and . . .

Then I reach the dragon's back leg. Underneath the shackle, blood glimmers darkly against its scales. Enormous claws rap against the tiles as it gobbles down its meal. *CLACK! CLACK! CLACK!* The sound causes every muscle in my body to shake. But somehow, I raise the key ring, careful to keep it from jingling. Torchlight flickers across the edges of the golden key. I bring it closer.

Slowly, cautiously.

The key is an inch from the hole when a shadow ripples across my feet. At the edge of my vision, I catch a glimpse of Prince Fred beside me. He's gone completely white. And that's when I notice. The dragon has stopped eating.

I turn my head a fraction to the left. Enough to see the creature's towering form, twisted back on itself. Long, scale-covered neck curved downward.

The dragon's looking right at me.

Prince Fred

The unblinking golden eyes stare at Kara for a thousand years. At least, that's how long it feels to me. Every second is an eternity. I hold my breath, afraid that the slightest disturbance might release the dragon's murderous wrath.

Kara is holding the golden key just beyond the rim of the keyhole. Her hand trembles.

A noise issues from deep within the dragon's throat. A low, steady growl. The dragon's dark lip curls back to reveal its huge, deadly teeth.

Then the creature's gaze shifts to the key in Kara's hand. A moment later, its eyes flick to the shackle around its leg. And then back to Kara.

The key.

The shackle.

Kara.

The dragon's golden gaze flicks back and forth. Until a look of understanding comes over its huge, scaly face.

Kara holds the key to its freedom.

The creature ceases growling. It stops baring its terrible teeth.

Kara's grip on the key tightens. And then she nudges it forward. Delicately sliding the key into the hole.

The dragon waits like an extremely large house pet. It's even wagging its tail.

With both hands, Kara turns the key.

CLICK!

My heart leaps. The shackle opens. The dragon lifts its leg and the massive steel restraint falls to the floor with an echoing clatter.

But the sense of relief lasts for only a moment. Because the dragon reacts to its newfound freedom by surging forward and chomping off Kara's head.

Kara

⁓

Lucky for me, Prince Fred's wrong. The dragon doesn't bite me. It *licks* me.

Just imagine a golden retriever licking your face. Now instead of a golden retriever, think of something a hundred times bigger—and covered in scales—with massive leathery wings flapping excitedly. And instead of just licking your face, imagine it licking your *entire body*—

Actually . . . *don't*. Because I can tell you from personal experience, it's the nastiest thing that's ever happened to me. One second, I'm terrified. The next, I'm covered in slobber.

Wet, sticky dragon slobber.

I guess that's a dragon's way of saying *Thanks for un-chaining me.*

But on the bright side, at least I still have my head. After licking me, the dragon hops high above us. Its wings pound the air. It soars happily around the vast chamber, doing figure eights around the pillars and performing somersaults.

The dragon circles around, casting one last grateful glance in our direction. And then it flaps away. Across the chamber and down a broad corridor, vanishing into the shadows.

When I turn back to Prince Fred, he's staring at me. Right then, it's tough to avoid feeling self-conscious. Gooey dragon saliva drips down my face and soaks into my clothes. My hair feels like it's been dipped in warm tapioca pudding.

I'm sure the prince will be disgusted. But instead, he steps forward and gives me a giant hug.

"I thought . . ." His voice quavers. "I thought you were dead."

"Nope," I say. "Just covered in dragon drool."

And now, so is he. Not that Prince Fred seems to mind. When he steps away, his clothes are all slick and globby. And he has a relieved smile on his face.

"Shall we open the door?" he asks.

"Let's."

Now that the chain is no longer attached to a dragon, it's easy enough to slide through the heavy supports. We circle the chain around—once, twice—until it's no longer sealing the door of the walk-in refrigerator closed.

I carefully set the chain on the floor and then stand up. I'm reaching for the handle when I feel sharp steel against my neck. A familiar voice speaks into my ear.

"Hello, little girl."

My breath catches. The Sorceress is standing beside me.

I don't know where she came from. Whether she snuck up on us or simply appeared out of nowhere. But there she is. Tall and dark, an eerie smile on her face. In her hand is a long silver knife. Its blade presses against my skin.

From the corner of my vision, I can see Prince Fred. He's directly behind the Sorceress, gripping the sword in both hands, moving silently forward.

He raises the sword.

Prepares to strike.

And then . . .

Nothing happens. He remains frozen with the sword above his head. As if someone put the prince on pause.

Fred's eyes flick from side to side. I can see him straining

249

to move. The muscles in his arms flex. A vein bulges on his forehead. His jaw tightens. But none of it does any good.

He's stuck. Sword clutched above his head. Like a statue.

And I don't need to guess who's to blame. Without taking her eyes off me, the Sorceress speaks.

"Did you really think you could sneak up on me, Prince?" Cruelty and amusement swim in the dark currents of her voice. "I would recognize your footfalls anywhere."

The Sorceress chuckles darkly.

"It's rather humorous, don't you think? For three years, I cast every spell imaginable upon the miniature doorway. And none of it worked. In the end, it wasn't wizardry that opened the door for me. It was *you*. You and your little friend."

The knife's blade presses harder against my neck.

"I suppose I owe you children a debt of gratitude," she says. "If it weren't for you, I would never have made it here. But how can I possibly thank you when you keep meddling in my plans?"

The Sorceress turns her dark gaze on me. A wave of goose bumps rises along my skin.

"I never thought one little girl could cause so many headaches. Escaping from my soldiers. Breaking into my castle. Freeing my hostage—*and* my dragon."

Her attention shifts back to the prince.

"And *you*." The Sorceress's tone curdles with disgust as she stares at Prince Fred. "The spoiled little worm who is destined to be king. Pampered, coddled, granted every luxury in the Royal Palace. Vain, selfish, arrogant. With a throne as your birthright. And why? Because the king and queen just *happen* to be your parents?"

Rage simmers in Prince Fred's eyes, but he's unable to attack, unable to reply, unable to do anything except stand there, frozen, and listen.

In a bitter tone, the Sorceress continues: "The truth—Prince Frederick the Fourteenth—is that you never had what it takes to be a king. True rulers do not inherit power. They *take* it!"

Torchlight flickers in her dark eyes. I'm more afraid than I've ever been.

"Soon I shall have dominion over both worlds. Not that either of you will live to see it. Pity I cannot kill you just yet, Prince. I suppose the little girl will have to do."

Prince Fred

I struggle against the Sorceress's spell. Grit my teeth. Strain every muscle in my body. But none of it works. I remained as I was before. Unmoving as a block of stone. With no choice but to stand, perfectly still, and watch Kara die.

At first, I don't notice the sounds. The flapping of giant wings. The echoing growl.

But it's impossible to miss the thunderous roar.

The noise ricochets across the vast chamber. Pillars shiver. The floor trembles.

And from the shadows of the broad corridor, the dragon reappears.

My body may have been frozen, but my brain is churning. What's the dragon doing here? Why return to the place of its captivity? Then I recall how we discovered the dragon. Locked away. Isolated. Ignored. Bleeding. Starved. Gnawing at its restraints.

All because of the Sorceress.

No doubt the dragon wants to escape. But it seems as though there's one thing it wants even more.

Revenge.

The enormous creature shoots through the chamber like lightning. A blur of wings and teeth and claws.

The Sorceress's eyes snap in the dragon's direction, her mouth twisting with fury. In the instant of distraction, Kara knocks the knife out of her hand and dashes away. The Sorceress makes no move to follow her. At the moment, she has a much bigger concern.

"Disloyal lizard!" she shrieks. "How dare you defy me!"

The Sorceress raises her free hand. From her fingers comes a burst of white light. The dragon twists into a barrel roll and the spell destroys a pillar instead.

"When I found you, you were a tangle of fabric." The Sorceress unleashes another blast of light and singes the dragon's tail. "I made you into an unstoppable beast! I gave you *life*! And I can take it away!"

The dragon opens its jaws. Fire blazes across the chamber. The Sorceress dodges the flames with remarkable speed.

Unfortunately, I can't do the same. Not while I'm under the Sorceress's spell. Utterly and horribly stuck.

A great tidal wave of fire is headed straight for me. But Kara gets to me first. She slams into me and the two of us topple sideways, behind a pillar. Fire blazes on all sides. I feel as though I've been tossed into an oven. My entire body swallowed by agonizing heat. And yet—when the fire ceases, Kara and I are still alive.

Kara grabs me by the shoulders, her eyes wide with concern. "Are you all right?"

I try to nod. Instead something very peculiar happens. My finger moves. It's just a twitch. Barely noticeable. But believe me . . . when you've been stuck in the same position for as long as I have, that finger twitch feels like cartwheeling across the room.

The Sorceress's spell. It's wearing off! This is what I want to say, but my mouth still isn't working. And instead, another finger moves.

I rejoice. Around me, the battle rages. The Sorceress and the dragon, locked in fierce combat. Flashes of white light. Flames spewing. Roaring and shrieking and flapping wings. But my concentration is elsewhere. All my attention is on something much closer. My foot. I focus, strain, push. And all of a sudden, I feel . . .

A toe wiggle.

It may not be much, but it's progress. Next I move another toe. And an eyelid. My lip. Another finger. An entire foot.

"Oh my gosh!" Kara whispers excitedly. "You're moving!"

I know! What a marvelous development!

At least—that's what I *try* to say. But the muscles controlling my mouth haven't fully returned to normal yet. The words come out all wrong.

"Brumble glugg!" I say. "Frruuump blubbmenn!"

Kara tilts her head, confused.

I apologize, I try to say. *I have not regained the capacity for basic human speech.*

But what comes out is: "Derp pllooooop. Eeewweee sloooog pleeeech."

"Uh . . . okay." Kara lifts me into an upright position. "Do you think you can stand up?"

I shall try my hardest, I attempt.

"Flooop. Yoooop," I say.

Kara releases her grip on me. I fall onto my face.

"Looks like standing isn't an option just yet." Kara lifts me up again, leaning my back against the pillar. "And I don't think we have time to wait for the spell to wear off."

She has a point. The battle between the Sorceress and the dragon is taking its toll on the castle. A blast of the Sorceress's spell rips a hole in the stone wall. Spinning in midair to avoid her attack, the dragon slams through a pillar. Tremors jolt the floor. A massive chunk of the ceiling breaks loose and lands a few feet away.

I make another attempt to stand. This time, more of my body reacts. My arms strain to push against the floor. My legs flex. And . . .

I flop sideways.

"Maybe I can carry you?" Kara says.

Excellent idea! I try to say.

"Gooob rumpp!" I actually say.

Kara brings her hands under my armpits and lifts. At the same time, I push with my legs. The two of us stagger out from behind the pillar.

The walk-in refrigerator is fifteen feet away. We begin moving toward it. Half stumbling, half walking. Slumping my head to the right, I gain a view of the Sorceress. She has her back to us. And by the look of it, she's nearly vanquished the dragon. The creature's tail has been severed.

Its right wing is badly burned. Its scales glisten with blood from at least a dozen wounds.

But the dragon isn't through fighting yet. It sweeps along the edge of the chamber, veering sideways to avoid another burst of terrible magic from the Sorceress. The creature opens its mouth, spewing flames. Fire crashes over stone walls and pillars. It blooms against the floor and collides with a large stack of boxes at the edge of the room. Each one marked with the same words:

HANDLE WITH CAUTION
HIGHLY EXPLOSIVE

"Oh no," Kara says.

"Blurph," I say.

Then the entire chamber explodes in flames.

Kara

I've seen plenty of explosions in movies. Blown-up cars, demolished buildings, alien spaceships crashing to earth. But nothing could prepare me for the real thing.

KA-BOOOOOM!

The blast is deafening. Imagine thunder erupting inside your brain. Now crank up the volume even higher. You're still nowhere close to the sound that rocks my eardrums.

The cavernous room is torn apart. Thick stone walls crumble like LEGO pieces. Massive pillars collapse. The floor shakes.

The world is falling apart. And I'm right in the middle of it. With a half-paralyzed prince hanging over my shoulder. We're trapped in the heart of Legendtopia. Surrounded by flames. There's no chance of making it out of the castle alive. Our only hope for survival is . . .

The walk-in refrigerator.

But with all the smoke and debris kicked up by the explosion, I've completely lost sight of the big metal box. I drag Prince Fred blindly one way, then another. We change course again and again. But no matter which direction we go, it's always wrong.

It's hopeless. I'm totally turned around. Unable to see anything. Lost in the chaos.

Burning-hot ashes rain down, searing my skin. My lungs are clogged with smoke. A massive chunk of the ceiling slams to the ground beside us.

Prince Fred slips from my grasp. The two of us collapse, coughing and clasping at our throats. Flames billow through the fog of smoke and debris. It feels like someone's turned the thermostat in the chamber to a thousand.

If the smoke doesn't suffocate us, we'll burn to death.

We came so close. This thought whispers through my fevered brain. *So close to reaching the walk-in refrigerator. So close to Heldstone.*

But not close enough. And now I'll never find my dad.

Through the smoldering gray smoke, I can just barely

see Prince Fred's face. I begin to say goodbye, but something stops me.

A movement in a pocket of my dress. A faint rustling.

It must be my phone. Probably another burst of texts from Marcy. Then I remember—my phone no longer works. And Marcy wouldn't be texting me, anyway—not while she's brainwashed by the Sorceress's spell.

I reach into a fold in my torn dress, where a pocket has been sewn into the hem. My fingers settle over something small and metal.

The owl necklace.

I can feel its wings flutter against the palm of my hand. The smoke must be getting to my brain. That's the only explanation. I've witnessed a lot of magic over the last couple of days, but the necklace isn't supposed to be a part of all that. It has nothing to do with the Sorceress. It was given to me by . . .

My dad.

My memory tumbles backward. To the night before my dad disappeared. *If you keep this necklace with you, it'll bring you closer to me.* What if he was trying to tell me something? Something I'm only just now beginning to realize?

My thoughts bounce like a Ping-Pong ball between three different random events . . .

. . . the field trip to Legendtopia yesterday, when my owl necklace got stuck in the waitress's hat . . .

. . . searching through the shoe box of Dad's old stuff with Prince Fred, discovering that my father visited Heldstone once before . . .

. . . moments when I thought I felt the silver owl faintly rustling against my skin and assumed it was just my imagination . . .

I can't shake the feeling that they're all connected. *But how?*

The silver owl flaps forward, tugging at the chain. I still don't know how any of this is happening—or why—but I *am* sure about one thing:

The owl wants me to follow it.

Grasping the chain with one hand, I reach for Prince Fred with the other. I wrap my arm around him and lift. Together we rise to our feet and begin staggering in the direction that the necklace leads us. Deeper into the chaos. Explosions, chunks of stone collapsing, waves of fire crashing all around us. The heavy clouds of smoke and debris make it impossible to see where we're going, but that doesn't matter now. All that matters is the owl. The tiny silver bird flaps persistently at the end of its chain. Our guide through the destruction.

As the prince and I stumble behind the necklace, Dad's words echo in my memory, again and again. *If you keep this necklace with you, it'll bring you closer to me.*

And then I see it. A faint outline up ahead. The walk-in refrigerator. The owl yanks toward it like a fly on a string. I trip over a crater in the floor, nearly losing my grip on the necklace. But now Prince Fred has gained more of his strength. And as I begin to fall, he strains to hold me up.

We keep moving. The fridge is getting closer. The two of us stagger the final few steps. With his free hand, Fred lunges for the door. Grasping the handle, he pulls it open. Fred and I dive into the gaping mouth of the walk-in fridge.

We're inside.

As I reach to close the door, I get one last glimpse of the destruction outside. There's no sign of the dragon. Maybe it managed to escape. More likely, it was immediately engulfed by the explosion. Ashes of the puppet it had once been.

Then something else grabs my attention. A dark silhouette, surrounded by smoke and fire. The Sorceress. The flames part like a curtain. For a moment, I can see her face. And the weird thing is . . . her expression is pure calm. Even though she's smack in the middle of an inferno, the Sorceress looks like she's meditating. Eyes closed. Lips moving slightly. As if whispering to herself. She casts her arms wide, like a bird spreading its wings. And then—

The Sorceress vanishes.

At least—that's the way it looks. With the pandemonium raging all around, it's impossible to know for sure. Maybe she was swallowed by the flames. Maybe the explosion blew her to smithereens.

Except that doesn't explain the shadow.

In the spot where the Sorceress was just standing, there's now a swirl of darkness. It reminds me of the cloud above Legendtopia. The slow-motion tornado. The dark mass of toxic magic leaking into the sky. But on a much smaller scale.

The serene expression on her face. The moving lips. Was the Sorceress whispering a spell? Did she just turn herself into a shadow?

There's no time to wonder about these questions. Another seismic crash rocks the castle. A swell of fire rushes toward us.

My grip tightens on the handle and I yank the refrigerator door closed.

But not before the shadow slips inside.

With the door sealed shut, the only light comes from a sliver at the bottom of the door. The fire outside casts a dim, red glow across the interior of the walk-in refrigerator. But even in the faint illumination, I swear I see it. A swirling cloud of darkness. For the flicker of an instant, it hangs before me.

Then it's gone.

Or maybe it was never there in the first place. In the dark fridge, it's impossible to be sure.

"Did you see it?" I scream. "Where'd it go?"

"What are you talking about?" Prince Fred's voice is slurred and unsteady, but at least he's forming whole words again. "See *what*?"

"The shadow!"

"I have no idea what you're talking about. Although to be honest, I'm more curious about *that*."

Fred points at the necklace in my hand. The little silver owl continues flapping at the end of its chain.

Prince Fred raises his eyebrows. "Why didn't you tell me your necklace is a Chasing Charm?"

"A *what*?"

Before he can respond, a blast rocks the walk-in refrigerator. The crash sends both of us stumbling. Heat radiates from all sides.

The prince screams over the roar outside. "The refrigerator won't withstand the destruction much longer!"

I have so many more questions. What really happened to the Sorceress? How did my necklace suddenly come to life? And what's a Chasing Charm? But they'll have to wait. The walk-in feels like it's melting.

"Follow me!" I yell.

Clenching the necklace, I let the owl guide us deeper into the metal box. The red glow from under the door fades. It's too dark to see where we're going, but that doesn't matter. The necklace knows the way.

The shock waves of another explosion ripple through the fridge. Boxes topple to the ground all around us. Moldy veggies rain down on me. The fridge is heating up like a humongous oven. The walls are simmering red. The color of boiling lava. Any second now, they're going to melt away.

The owl is flapping so hard now, I'm worried it'll break loose from its chain. I can't see it any longer, but I can feel the direction it leads us.

It'll bring you closer to me. Dad's musical accent reverberates in my mind like an inspirational motto. *Closer to me.*

Before long, I spot something up ahead. The glimmering, flickering light of a torch.

"We're getting close!" I scream over the roar of destruction outside. "Just a little farther!"

Fred shoves aside a couple of boxes. We keep moving. The heat's becoming unbearable. Hair clings to my forehead. Sweat drips into my eyes. When I swipe it away, I notice the walls are brick now. The floor is cobblestone. And ahead of us is the door.

The miniature door.

The door to Prince Fred's world.

The door to my father.

I turn the handle and push it open. A shadow flickers at the edge of my vision. And for an instant, I'm sure I see it again. The black shadow, sweeping through the opening. But when I turn to get a better look, it's vanished.

There's no time to wonder about what I saw—or *didn't* see. A terrible bellow echoes through the passageway behind me. The sound of metal ripping apart. The walk-in refrigerator disintegrating. I open the door the rest of the way, and we stagger out of one world and into another.

Prince Fred

Kara slams the door closed.

For a very long moment, neither of us speaks. Everything around us is perfectly silent. The room is cool, but my hair and my clothes are soaked with sweat.

For the first time, I glance at my surroundings. We're back in the Chamber of Wizardry. Back in Heldstone. Home.

My gaze falls on Kara. Her mangled ball gown is covered with gray ash and scarred by burns. In one hand she holds the necklace. The tiny owl flaps its silver wings, yanking at the chain.

"How is this possible?" The words tremble as they leave

her lips. "How does this necklace know the way to your world?"

"It's called a Chasing Charm," I say. "At the moment of its creation, the owl was placed under a spell."

"What kind of spell?"

I consider this for a moment. Finally, I settle on an explanation. "Do you have ducks in your world?"

Kara gives me a confused look.

"Ducks?" I repeat. "Do they exist on Urth?"

"Yeah. But what does that have to do with anything?"

"When a duck is born, it forms a bond with the first living thing that it sees. If you're there at the moment a duck hatches from its egg, it will think of *you* as its mother—"

Kara taps her foot impatiently. "Thanks for the biology lesson. Would you please get to the point?"

"A Chasing Charm is like a baby duck. It forms a bond between an ordinary object"—I gesture to the silver owl—"and the first person who comes into contact with it. In the case of your necklace, I'm guessing that bond was formed with—"

"My dad," Kara whispers.

"Precisely. For as long as your necklace exists, it will abide by a single mission. To return to your father."

"But I've had this necklace for, like, three years. Why did it only start working now?"

"Because it was waiting."

"For what?"

"The right moment."

Kara stares at her necklace, bewilderment swimming in her features. "There were times when I was *sure* I could feel the owl moving. But I assumed it was just my mind playing tricks on me."

"Most Chasing Charms are quite basic. They can be purchased for a few coins from any third-rate witch or wizard at the black marketplace. Parents get them as toys for their children. They'll follow the kids across the house. Any farther than that, and the bond flickers away. But there are *some* Chasing Charms . . ."

I turn my gaze to the little owl. Its silver wings flap up and down, pulling the necklace tight like a leash.

"Some Chasing Charms are much more powerful," I say. "Their bond can stretch across endless distances. And they can be clever, too. Able to devise complex strategies for finding the way back. Such a remarkable Chasing Charm is extremely rare. It must've been crafted by an extremely skilled magician."

"Like the Sorceress?"

I nod. "She's the most skilled of all magicians."

Kara's brown eyes ignite, darting around the Chamber of Wizardry. "This room is, like, the Sorceress's workshop, right?"

I nod again.

"Okay, so . . ." Kara's voice quickens. "We know that my dad came to Heldstone twice. We found his work order in my shoe box where I keep all his old stuff. Proof that he inspected the refrigerator two days before he disappeared for good."

My brain works to keep up with the pace of Kara's words. "What're you saying?"

"I'm saying, the first time my dad came here, he walked through *this* door." Kara points to the miniature wooden doorway. "Into *this* room. The Sorceress's room. He's a curious guy. He must've done some looking around. Which is how he found—"

"Your necklace." Understanding dawns on me. "The Chasing Charm."

"Exactly! He was the first person who came into contact with the necklace. He became the duck's mommy!"

"In a manner of speaking, yes."

"After that first visit to Heldstone, he returned to my world. He brought the necklace with him. And he gave it to me. By that point, he must've known it was magical."

I tilt my head. "What makes you think that?"

"Because of something he told me." Kara peers over my shoulder, as though looking into a memory from long ago. "*If you keep this necklace with you, it'll bring you closer to me.*' That's what he said when he gave me the necklace. And that's exactly what the Chasing Charm does. It leads me to him."

Sunlight streams into the Chamber of Wizardry through a colored-glass window. Outside, it must be mid-afternoon. The same time as Urth. As I stare into the red and blue beams of illumination, a realization stirs in my mind.

"I don't think any of this was an accident," I say.

Kara scrunches her brow. "What do you mean?"

"I mean, when you stumbled through the miniature door the first time . . . it wasn't just a random event."

Kara casts a glance at the small wooden door beside us. "Of course it was. It's not like I was *looking* for the door."

"Perhaps you weren't," I say. "But the Chasing Charm *was.*"

"That's impossible. I didn't even *have* the necklace at the time. It was stuck in the waitress's hat."

"Exactly."

Kara exhales loudly. "I think maybe you bumped your head back in Legendtopia, 'cause you're not making any sense."

"A powerful Chasing Charm can use complex strategies for finding its master. Strategies that can even stretch beyond our own comprehension."

"Okay. And?"

I take a breath and try a different approach. "Tell me again how you found the miniature doorway."

"I was hiding in the walk-in refrigerator."

"But why were you hiding?"

"Because of the—"

Kara's jaw drops.

"The necklace," she whispers. "It got caught in the waitress's hat. I went after it—"

"And instead you found the door to my world."

Kara shakes her head slowly. "I figured it was a coincidence."

"The Chasing Charm *wanted* you to get up from your table. It *wanted* you to go after the waitress. On some level, it must've known that would set off a course of events that would lead here."

"But nothing's *that* powerful!"

I give Kara a long look. "What about the Sorceress? She was able to create an army of ruthless minions. To transform your entire town. To breathe life into ordinary objects and cause animals to talk. To brainwash people into becoming her loyal subjects." I shudder at the magnitude of the Sorceress's dark magic. "If she could do all that—in a single day—imagine the kind of spell she could cast on a Chasing Charm."

Kara stares at the little silver owl. A link to her father. And a relic of the Sorceress's evil enchantment.

I can see how troubling all this is. Placing a hand on her shoulder, I say, "At least we can take comfort in the knowledge that the Sorceress is dead."

A look of doubt creeps across Kara's features. "I'm not so sure."

"There's no way she survived the fire."

"I know what I saw. One second she was there, surrounded by flames. And the next—there was this . . . shadow."

I wave her suggestion away. "There was fire everywhere. And smoke. Your eyes were probably just playing tricks on you."

"Maybe you're right," Kara replies. But judging by her grim expression, I get the feeling she doesn't believe it.

"Let's focus on the positive. We survived. We made it to Heldstone. Now we can begin the search for your father."

I reach into the pocket of my ash-covered pants and remove the scrap of parchment. My eyes fall on a couplet:

People flocked, far and wide, to listen
To the fantastical tales of the Elektro-Magician.

"We know he's been captured by the Thurphenwald tribe," I say. "They're keeping him as a carnival attraction."

"And we also have *this*." Kara nods at the silver owl, its metal wings flapping at the end of its silver leash. "It'll lead us to him."

"But first, we have more immediate concerns to deal with."

Kara clenches her jaw. "What's more immediate than finding my dad?"

"I've been missing for a full day now. My mother and father are probably worried sick. We can't begin our search until I've assured them that I am safe. And as for you—"

"What *about* me?"

"You're new to this world. How am I supposed to explain your presence?"

Kara shrugs. "Maybe . . . maybe I can hide."

"It's rather difficult to hunt down a nomadic tribe *and* hide at the same time. I'm afraid you have no choice. You will need to become a part of this world. Learn the customs. Blend in."

"I can do that."

"It's not so simple," I warn. "Of course, *I* was able to convince the inhabitants of your world that I was a completely normal twelve-year-old boy—"

Kara snorts. "*Nobody* thought you were normal."

"Well, it's going to be ten times as difficult for you. Trust me. Our mission will take longer. We'll have to travel great distances to find your father. We'll encounter strange creatures, unfamiliar cultures, perilous landscapes. And all along the way, you'll need to convince everyone you meet that you're a native of Heldstone. Because if anyone becomes suspicious—"

"I know," Kara says. "It'll make it harder to find my dad."

"That's correct."

Kara's features harden with resolve. And even though neither of us speaks, I can tell we're sharing the same thought. . . .

This is only the beginning of our journey.

Don't miss the next LEGENDTOPIA book,
THE SHADOW QUEEN.

Acknowledgments

Epic thanks go to the following:

Sarah Burnes, my exceptional agent, for your thoughtful guidance and passion. And for recommending I reread *The Magician's Nephew.* The White Witch is seriously scarier than I remember.

Logan Garrison, for taking a chance on my first manuscript and being there ever since.

Will Roberts and *Rebecca Gardner,* for sharing my books with the rest of the world, and everyone else at the *Gernert Company.*

Wendy Loggia, my brilliant editor (on four books now!), for being my trusted guide in the dark and scary forest that stands between the first draft and the finished book.

Beverly Horowitz, for the generous support and kind attention you've shown me and my books.

Bobbie Ford, for sharing my books with booksellers—and your mom!

The amazing team at Delacorte Press/Random House Children's Books, in particular *Krista Vitola, Nicole DuFort, Nicole Gastonguay, Adrienne Waintraub, Lisa McClatchy, Dandy Conway, Brenda Conway, Kate Sullivan,* and *Dominique Cimina.*

The unimpeachable copy editors, for making sure I use words like "unimpeachable" correctly.

All the educators, librarians, principals, administrators, PTAs, and *parents* I've met doing school visits around the country. Your dedication to kids and reading is truly legendary.

Independent booksellers, for your passion, commitment, and incredible love of books.

Michael and Irmtrud Schlör; Karin Schlör and *Kalle Geis;* and *Zenta Englert,* for showing me a great number of castles, even though I'm a little disappointed that we never came across any trolls, ogres, or dragons.

My brother, *Evan Bacon,* for being an endless source of intelligence, creativity, and hilarity.

My parents, *Jamie and Terry Bacon,* for providing me

with an enchanted upbringing in which both education and imagination were encouraged.

And finally, my wife, *Eva Bacon*, for trusting that I was a writer before I fully trusted it myself, for being German in your honesty and American in your encouragement, and for all the magic you've brought into my life.